GRANDPA TALES

Edited by Lalita Iyer

Illustrated by
Vidya Gopal

SCHOLASTIC
New York Toronto London Auckland
Sydney New Delhi Hong Kong

Published by Scholastic India Pvt. Ltd.
A subsidiary of Scholastic Inc., New York, 10012 (USA).
Publishers since 1920, with international operations in Canada, Australia, New Zealand, the United Kingdom, India, and Hong Kong.

For information regarding permission, write to:
Scholastic India Pvt. Ltd.
A-27, Ground Floor, Sigma Centre
Infocity-1, Sector 34, Gurgaon 122001 (India)

First edition: May 2018
Reprint; August 2018

ISBN-13: 978-93-5275-497-7

Printed at Sanat Printers, Kundli, Haryana.

EDITOR'S NOTE

Grandparents are funny little things. The first funny thing about them is that they get littler as they get older, so, technically, it is very easy for children to get their way around them as they never give a "I am the boss of you" vibe which generally parents tend to do. Also, grandparents are convenient messengers when you want something from your parents but don't know how to ask. Grandmothers and grandfathers have their uses, apart from being cuddle toys. This book is stories of, about and from grandpas—the things they do, the lives they live, the people they are.

The last volume of grandparent stories was full of grandma tales and several grandpas and their fans rose in protest, so we decided that this time grandpas will get the limelight. However, some grandmas did sneak in, as they believe grandpas are up to no good when left alone. I tend to agree.

Lalita Iyer

CONTENTS

GRANDPA'S EXTREMELY EXAGGERATED ESCAPADE

Natasha Sharma

My father's thrilling tales of his days growing up in boarding schools in Dehradun and Mussoorie are the sort that leave you open-mouthed and goggle-eyed, sucked into his descriptive, detailed and spiced-up telling. We lapped them up as children. Now I have children, and my grandfather continues to enthral them.

'We're sleeping with Nanu and no one else! No one tells stories like he does!'

'What? Seriously?' I ask.

But they are already tucked in bed with him, arms around his round frame, clinging to him like puppies, waiting for the next great "real life" adventure.

Every now and then I stick my ear through the door and listen in. The stories have grown wilder, feature nuttier teachers and have an increasingly swashbuckling representation of Nanu in his days of youth. It must be that rounder belly that has given him more space for spinning stuff inside!

The fattened-up version of one of these numerous stories, heard with my ear at the door and presented with a touch of my own garnish, is Grandpa's Extremely Exaggerated Escapade.

***

'We had been trekking for fourteen days.'

'Are you telling us the story about the master who fed you only jalebi in milk and dal moth on the hike after which you had the loosies?' ask the children.

'No no. This is a new one! Now listen! We'd been trekking for fourteen days. We haven't ended up at Everest, have we? I asked my three friends. We were completely lost, though not one of us would admit it.'

'Did you check the GPS?' ask the children.

'There was no GPS she-pee-es back then. You techy kids need to learn how to manage without gadgets. We had maps.'

'Then why were you lost?'

'We weren't good at reading maps.'

'You didn't call home?'

'There was no phone booth anywhere! We were in the mountains!'

'Oh, so the mobile wasn't picking up any signal?'

'There were no mobiles! We didn't have

anything on us to help us get in touch with people back home. There was nothing to be done other than continue walking till someone or something found us. Hopefully it wouldn't be a leopard.'

'No mobiles!' yelps one.

'A leopard!' yelps the other.

'Yes, a leopard. There were many wild animals around. Leopards, bears, pythons and more such dangerous creatures. But we were brave fellows. Brave but very tired. If my shoulders could speak, they would have yelped "Ow!" If my ankles had a voice, they would have wailed "Aargh!" If my calves could utter a word, they would have squealed "Ouch!" Since all these body parts depended on the one mouth I had, it opened in an elongated "OUCHHH!"

'Fortunately, at the end of that long "ouch", we heard a rumble. It sounded more like a choke. Surely you've heard that sound when someone has put their hands around your neck and is trying to choke you and all you can say is "KHWWWAAACCK!"'

'No, Nanu, we haven't.'

'Really? I once had two hands around my neck making me go "KHWWWAAACCK" but I was able to use my special twist and slide tackle to free myself. But that makes for another story. And don't you ever try and put your hands around anyone's neck unless they are around the neck of a piece of butter chicken. Even then I'd leave it alone. The neck is Nani's favourite piece and if you eat it up, she'll be worse than a leopard that has just had a toddler draw flowers around its spots with a permanent marker. So what was I saying? Ah yes! We heard a choke, a stutter, a screech and then a rumble. A truck appeared, straining its way up the steep mountain road.

'We stood there with our thumb out, trying to hitch a ride even though we had been told many times by our parents, "Never. Ever. Hitch a ride. They might kidnap you. We really don't have money to pay a ransom. And we might just leave you there." We hitched a ride. You must never ever do that. Say that to me now.'

'Yes, Nanu. We will never ever hitch a ride. But you did, didn't you?'

'Yes. But I was foolish. You are smart. At that time, anything was preferable to walking another step.

'Unfortunately it turned out that the truck driver was a bit of a grumpy person and insisted we sit at the back of the truck.

'Fortunately it was a big truck.

'Unfortunately it was full of potatoes. Raw potatoes. Hard as stones. Piled high to the top. Bumping around under our bottoms. We clung onto whatever bit of railing we could find, holding our rucksacks and each other for dear life.

' "Getting a ride was fortunate," said a friend as he flew a foot in the air and landed with a bump.

'The truck driver seemed to be in the maddest rush to get to the potato market. Perhaps it was the last day of a potato sale. Perhaps people were going to stop eating potatoes from the next day and this was the last day to sell them. Perhaps there was a great potato pie festival, or even better, a french fries festival at the destination …'

'… Perhaps this was dinner for a potato-powered superhero and the truck needed to get there in time for the world to be saved?' adds one child.

'… Perhaps there was a body of a kidnapped child who had hitchhiked just like you under that gigantic pile of potatoes, and the truck driver had to get to his destination and dispose it off before it raised a stink!' adds another.

'What morbid imagination! I wonder from where you get that. Yes, the possibilities were endless, but there was no way we could discuss any of this. One fellow had his teeth sunk into a potato to prevent them from rattling and breaking. The other fellow was leaning over the side and throwing up. The ride was making him nauseous. The sight of no embankment anywhere—just a straight drop all the way to the valley floor—made him feel worse as he leaned out. He did this at a most unfortunate moment, just as the truck swerved around a particularly sharp bend in the road. The fellow who was sick suddenly acquired anti-gravity powers. His legs flew up in the air and he almost fell off the side of the truck. His fingers barely clung onto the edge.

‘I leapt forward and managed to hook my fingers into his belt while digging my feet deep into the potatoes to get a grip. The potato-mouthed fellow hooked his hands around my waist. With every ounce of muscle I had developed over the last term as a member of the boxing team at school (I did tell you about my boxing), I held onto that belt, praying that it had a strong buckle. Rivers of sweat poured down my face. My heart beat twice as fast as it usually did. My muscles grew and popped up like eggs, thanks to all the eggs I’d been eating that term. I hope you’ve been eating your eggs.

‘Yes Nanu,’ chirp the two, nodding their heads like angels without a sliver of guilt for having lied blatantly.

‘Fortunately, the truck driver on that rare occasion looked into his side view mirror. The sight of a flying boy being pulled by an egg-muscled boy being pulled by a potato-mouthed boy made him press down hard on the brake.

'I had just managed to get my flying friend back over the edge when the screeching, slow motion halt made him fall flat on me. The potato-mouthed fellow ended up swallowing half the potato and promptly looked green. I rolled the flying fellow off and whacked the potato fellow on his back since he was now going "KHWAAACCCKKK!" By the time the two had got back a flicker of life into themselves, the truck driver had walked around to the back. He yelled, "NIKLO! OUT! If you die, I'll be held responsible."

'There we were, still lost, but had covered a fair bit of distance. However, we had no idea in which direction we should go. The truck driver had driven off before we could ask him for further directions.

'Fortunately we spotted a path that left the main road and seemed to cut across the mountain. A shortcut was welcome.

'We trudged on, and after two hours, we finally agreed that we were even more lost than before. The mountain seemed to look different as well, for there was sparse vegetation, loose rocks and soil in a rutted path along its edge. There was no road anymore. That's when we heard the first loud BOOM!'

'Boom?' asked the children.

'BOOM! BOOM! BOOM! Something seemed to be blasting around us. Booms and crashes meant we had to go investigate. If you hear booms and crashes, you must walk in the other direction.'

'But Nanu, you didn't.'

'I was young and foolish, but you are smart. Anyway, we finally spotted a bunch of men in the distance wearing yellow hard hats. They were waving their arms around like crazy people and doing this strange dance, jumping up and down. We walked closer and realised they were yelling at us. "STOP! STOP! DUCK! DUCK!"

'A friend asked, "Why are they so excited about ducks?"

'While we looked around for the unlikely sight of a duck in such a dry and rocky place, we heard the men scream louder. "DUCK! DYNAMITE!"

' "Did he say dynamite?" asked a brighter friend, just as a BOOM much louder than the earlier ones shook the mountain above us.

' "DYNAMITE!" the four of us squawked, terrified now.

'We flattened ourselves against the face of the mountain, clinging on like leeches to a leg. I know how hard they can cling. I used to come back with twenty leeches on each leg when I worked in the tea gardens.'

"Twenty lee...leee...leeches? Didn't that hurt?"

'Leeches? Of course not! They clean up your blood. Sprinkle salt on them and watch them fall off once they've done their job. So, the BOOMs of dynamite continued above us. They were building a road and cutting a path into the mountain and we had walked smack bang into the middle of it. Loose rocks tumbled down around us. One rock hit my friend's tin mug hanging off his rucksack. The mug accompanied the stones all the way down the hill, its distant clanging reminding us of how far we could fall.

'Finally the blasting stopped. Still clinging to the rocks, now like monkeys, we found our way to safety. The men who had been shouting at us earlier almost hung us upside down. "Get out of here! If you'd died, we'd have been held responsible for idiots like you."

'We eventually made it to a tiny town a few days later after a night of floating mattresses (tomorrow's story) and another night of horse poo (day after's story). That's it for today. Good night!'

***

The room immediately explodes in a flurry of moans and pleas for another story … just a short one … about the housemaster who climbed the roof of the school. As I'm closing the door, echoes of my own voice seem to carry over to the room with my children.

'Our school isn't as exciting as yours was, Nanu,' they cry.

'Put away your gadgets and head outdoors,' says the grandfather. 'Life will be a real adventure.'

VITAMIN M

Asha Nehemiah

'I wish,' said Ravi's mother, hurriedly putting some green, red and orange tablets on a saucer, 'that somebody would invent a memory vitamin. They could call it Vitamin M and we could give it to old people to help their memories improve.'

'Shh, Grandpa'll hear you,' said Ravi, pointing to the frail old figure sitting in the rocking chair, holding the newspaper inches from his nose to read it.

'Don't worry. I doubt Grandpa can hear me. He doesn't hear too well, or see too well, or remember too well these days. I'm glad that you're on holiday from today and can look after him. Last month was …' she stopped and shuddered at the memory.

It was only last month that Ravi's grandfather had come to live with them because he was getting too old to live on his own. It had been a difficult month, with Grandpa admitted in the hospital because he had absentmindedly taken a double dose of his medicines. He had also given them several anxious moments by getting lost when he had gone for a walk on his own and forgotten the way back home.

Grandpa had got very upset when his daughter, Ravi's mother, insisted that he shouldn't go out alone again. 'I'll have you know, Vidya, my dear,' he had told his daughter with a trace of the firmness that had been a natural part of his job as a lawyer, 'that I've been looking after myself for the better part of my seventy five years. After your mother died ten years ago, I took over her duties as well, and was cooking, shopping and keeping house too. First you force me to come and live with you in this poky little flat in this horrible, crowded city and then you think you have the right to forbid me to go out on my own!'

Grandpa hated the noise and bustle of city life and when they were on their own, would often speak longingly to Ravi of his small brick house in town. 'Such a wonderful place. With that big mango tree in the garden. So quiet, that at dusk, you can even hear a leaf drop!' But then Grandpa had slipped and fallen in the garden late one evening while he was pottering around, and he lay outside all night because there was no one to help him up. That was a month ago and it made Ravi's mother lock up the tiny brick house and bring Grandpa to live with them.

'Whatever happens, Ravi, you're not to let Grandpa go out on his own. It's too dangerous,' she instructed her son, adding details of the medicines to be given to Grandpa after lunch. Turning to her father, she said, 'I'm off to work, Appa. Ravi will be here to look after you. He's on holiday from today.'

Ravi winced at the too loud tone his mother used when speaking to Grandpa, as though she was speaking to a child who couldn't hear or understand too well. Grandpa continued to rock gently and gave no sign that he had heard her at all.

'Don't worry, Amma,' Ravi promised, looking at his mother's anxious face and feeling sorry for her. 'You go to work. Grandpa'll be fine at home with me.'

'Shall we play chess or watch the cricket match on TV, Grandpa?' Ravi asked after his mother left. Grandpa played a great game of chess, very cool and cunning, and Ravi found that his own game had significantly improved ever since Grandpa had come to live with them. 'That's the opening move Kasparov made when he played against the computer,' he would tell Ravi as he moved a piece. Or 'You're making the same mistake that Bobby Fischer made in his historic match against Spasky.'

How can he remember all those thousands of chess games and still forget the names of people he meets often? Ravi wondered.

'Just set up the chess board, Ravi,' Grandpa put his paper down. 'I'll walk to the corner of the street to see whether the Tamil newspaper has arrived.'

'Appa usually buys you the Tamil paper on his way home! But if you want it right now, I'll buy it for you,' Ravi offered.

'I hope you're not going to be as tiresome as your mother, Ravi. Treating me like a baby. Has she told you not to let me go out on my own? Told you to keep me a prisoner here, has she?' Grandpa suddenly looked suspicious.

Ravi looked guilty for a moment, then quickly recovered to say loyally, 'Of course not, Grandpa. Amma would never treat you like a baby. Or as a prisoner.'

'Good,' said Grandpa craftily, 'then you'll have no objection to me going out.'

He picked up his beautiful shiny black mahogany walking stick with a brass handle carved in the shape of an eagle's head. He put on his bright yellow cap and declared, 'I'll be back home before you have set up the board, Ravi.'

He set off, twirling his walking stick jauntily, leaving Ravi in a fix. His grandfather would feel hurt if he insisted on accompanying him, and his mother would be furious if she knew Ravi had let him go out on his own.

He heard the elevator door shut as Grandpa went down. Ravi decided he would follow Grandpa secretly, at a safe distance, to make sure he came to no harm.

He ran out of the building just in time, to see Grandpa's yellow cap disappearing round the corner. Grandfather's first stop was the children's park where he bought himself a paper cone of peanuts and settled on a bench watching the children play. Ravi, feeling very foolish, had to crouch behind a bush trimmed in the shape of an elephant to avoid being seen. He felt even more foolish when a small child came up to him and asked, 'Are you playing hide and seek? I can show you a better place to hide.'

'Shh, shhh,' was all Ravi could say before he felt a shadow fall over him. An enormous voice boomed, 'How dare you shoo my child? Who are you?' It was the little boy's mother.

'Shh shh,' Ravi repeated to the massive lady.

'I'll shhh you, you rude boy!' said the large lady, picking up her umbrella threateningly. The ultimate humiliation was when Ravi had to crawl out of the park on all fours, ducking behind the benches, creeping behind the bushes, thanking his lucky stars that Grandpa hadn't heard the commotion and spotted him.

Grandpa's next stop was the tea stall and this time Ravi took position behind a big banyan tree to watch him, feeling most embarrassed when the vendors sitting under the tree gave him quizzical looks.

'This area is booked by us,' said one old lady who was selling plastic combs, in the same tone she might have used had she been asked to address a gathering without being given a loudspeaker. 'There's no room for any new vendor.'

'Shhh. Don't talk so loudly. Do I look as though I'm selling anything?' Ravi asked her.

'Who's talking loudly?' said the old lady, raising her voice just enough for Ravi to hear her had she been talking to him from across the city.

'Who are you accusing of talking loudly? And that too, hiding behind the tree. Who are you hiding from?' another vendor selling ribbons and clips asked. She too was one of those lucky ones who would never ever require a megaphone.

'Yes. Are you talking about one of us?' asked another vendor as a group of them surrounded Ravi.

'Oh, all right!' Ravi conceded defeat and moved to duck behind a shiny silver car, peering through the windows to keep an eye on Grandpa. Grandpa took his time sipping a sugary cup of tea (he was forbidden sugar at home), then ate two bananas (another banned item), then slurped an ice cream bought from the cart. (Mother would faint if she saw this!)

Ravi himself felt hot, bothered and faint by the time Grandpa finished his snack. His heart thudded anxiously when he saw Grandpa zigzagging through the traffic as he crossed the road. He shut his eyes in panic when he heard a screech of brakes and opened them just in time to see Grandpa entering the barber shop. Now Grandpa was as bald as a table tennis ball, so Ravi decided that a closer look was in order. He crossed the road, first looking left and then right and then hurriedly ducked into the shop next to the barber shop … only to be evicted a moment later amidst a volley of feminine shrieks because it happened to be a ladies hairdressing salon.

Just as well that I got thrown out, thought Ravi, because he spotted Grandpa making his way briskly towards the bus stop and—oh no—boarding the first bus that stopped there.

Sprinting for the bus and jumping onto it seconds before it started would have deterred a lesser detective, but not Ravi, who was panting as he struggled for a place in the bus. He could see Grandpa's yellow cap somewhere in the front. It was warm inside, so Grandpa took off his cap to reveal … a full head of grey hair! Ravi was startled. Surely

Grandpa wouldn't have bought a wig at the barber shop, he thought, pushing his way to the front of the bus to confront the cap wearer. The person was a stranger! He was wearing a white dhoti and shirt, which was Grandpa's standard attire, and a yellow cap exactly like Grandpa's. But wait, the cap had a coffee stain on its rim just like Grandpa's!

'Grandpa's cap!' Ravi couldn't help exclaiming. The stranger grinned pleasantly and told Ravi that a kind old gentleman in the barber shop had insisted that he take his cap because it was such a hot day. That was typical of Grandpa, always generous. But where was Grandpa?

Ravi went back to the barber shop. Grandpa wasn't there. He wasn't at the park either. Ravi was frantic. After all, his mother had left him in charge of Grandpa. He tried calling her first and then his father, but both numbers were busy. Sick with worry, Ravi went home wondering whether Grandpa would be able to find his way back.

To his great delight and relief, the first thing he heard when he opened the front door was the gentle snoring of Grandpa in his bedroom. He knelt down near the bed and put his cheek against the old man's face. Grandpa's thin, wrinkled skin had more creases than a map had lines. Grandpa smelled of eucalyptus ointment and shaving cream. Ravi suddenly felt overcome with affection for him and gave him a hug, but Grandpa only grunted in his sleep. He decided not to question Grandpa because then he would have to reveal that he had been following him.

'What did you two do today?' asked Ravi's mother when she got back from the office.

'I had a quiet morning, but I don't know about Ravi. He just disappeared instead of staying at home to look after me like you asked him to,' answered Grandpa coolly, while Ravi just nodded in surprise.

Grandpa had another surprise for Ravi. A gift-wrapped parcel!

'But Appa, Ravi's birthday was three months ago. Have you forgotten?' exclaimed Ravi's mother impatiently.

'No. But, you know, I always give a gift to every child in the house on *my* birthday. Have you forgotten?' countered Grandpa very seriously.

Ravi's mother flushed red and darted a stricken look at the calendar on which she had, at the beginning of the year, circled that day's date in red and written "Appa's birthday" beside it. There was a gift for her too, and for Ravi's father as well, for Grandpa still considered them his "children".

Grandpa turned to Ravi's father who had just walked into the room. 'My daughter needs some Vitamin M, I think. For her memory.' Ravi's mother flushed a darker shade of red and her husband looked confused.

Ravi unwrapped his gift to find a thick, hardback book, *The Best Detective Stories.*

'Great stories, Ravi. You can pick up some really good tips on how to be a detective. How to avoid getting fooled when one is trailing a suspect, for instance,' Grandpa advised Ravi.

'I don't think he wants to be a detective, do you, Ravi?' asked his father, looking even more confused.

'I haven't decided yet,' answered Ravi, because he was too busy trying to decide whether the twinkle in Grandpa's eye was an innocent gleam or a mischievous one.

Vitamin M is a story based on an incident from my life. My younger brother, who was around 10 years at the time, had read all about detectives "following" people. One evening he decided to try out some of the tricks he'd read about. He followed my grandfather on his evening walk, ducking into alleys to avoid being spotted. He was thrilled when he actually made a startling discovery. My grandfather, who was not supposed to eat sweets for health reasons, was seen tucking into rasgullas and gulab jamuns at the sweet shop round the corner when he though no one was watching. Somehow, this incident came back to me years later and found its way into my story Vitamin M. Of course, I changed several things around to make the story more dramatic and funny. The grandfather in the story is based on my own grandfather, who was a criminal lawyer and hated leaving his own home in Chennai to come and live with us.

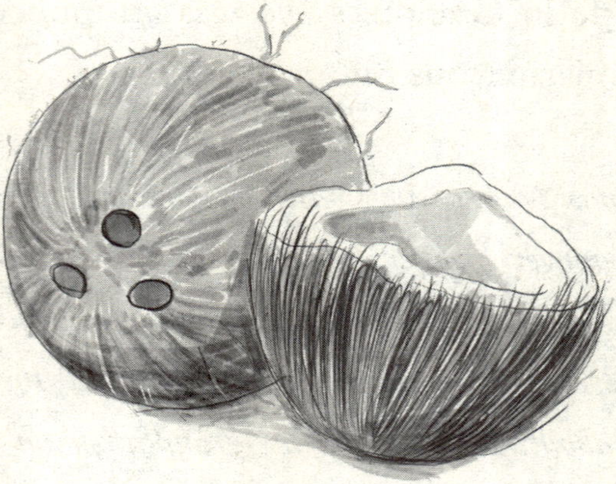

How the Coconut Tree Came To Be

Binu Sivan

Hundreds of thousands of years ago, a little girl lived in a small hut by a lake. Her parents and elder brothers were often busy. The little girl, Cheenu, would help her mother around the house and in the vegetable patch next to their hut. They were very poor, and their hut was falling apart. Her parents were often worried about how they were going to survive the rainy season next year if their house kept falling apart like this.

Cheenu was a happy child. She helped her parents as much as any good kid. When she was done, she would run down to the lake and dive in and swim for hours. 'How cool and soft the water is!' she sighed as she floated on it.

She loved the ducks and the fish that lived in the water. One day, as she was swimming, she saw a long shadow slide through the water. Cheenu was worried. She was quite sure that there were no snakes in the lake, but one could never say. She dove underwater and swam with the creature and saw that its head was quite large and it had something that looked like fins. This could not be a snake. She reached out and touched it and felt a sharp pain that nearly knocked her out. What was that! Cheenu leapt out of the water in shock and ran back home. She did not tell anyone about this strange creature, though.

The next day she ran back to the lake as soon as she could. She looked carefully into the water for the long shadow but could not see it. As she was stepping into the water, she saw the creature swimming around a rock. It was looking at her. She felt that it had been waiting for her. She swam to the creature, being careful not to touch it, and swam in circles around the rock with it. This became their daily routine after that.

After a few days, the creature even allowed her to touch it, and their daily swimming session became the highlight of their day. Every day, before she returned home, she would gently pat the creature goodbye. Initially she was secretly scared of feeling the sharp pain again, but soon she started relaxing and even forgot about the pain.

One day, as Cheenu left the lake, the creature also swam out and rested on the bank of the lake. Cheenu was surprised. She had never seen any fish do that! Suddenly, in front of her eyes, the creature transformed into a handsome young man.

He smiled and said, 'I am Ambu, the God of eels. You have been a very good friend and I would like to remain by your side forever. But it is time for me to leave you.'

Despite her shock, Cheenu managed to ask Ambu why he wanted to leave.

'My time on Earth is up. I have to return where I came from. But I want to leave you a gift by which you can always remember me. For that you will have to do exactly what I ask you to do.'

Cheenu was willing to do anything to be able to keep the memory of her friend alive. She agreed.

Ambu turned back towards the lake and told her, 'Tomorrow when you open the door of your hut, I will be lying nearby in my eel form. You must take an axe and cut off my head and bury it near where I am lying.'

Cheenu was shocked by Ambu's request, but before she could say or ask anything, he dived into the lake and swam away.

Cheenu could not sleep at all that night. Early the next morning, before even her mother woke up, Cheenu quietly opened the door and sneaked out. About seven feet away lay Ambu, the eel, and it was looking at her as though telling her, 'Do as you promised!'

Taking a deep breath, Cheenu got the axe, raised it and hacked off the eel's head as she had promised. She cried through it all. She then buried the head right there. But from that day on Cheenu did not feel like swimming in the lake. She would sit by the lake for hours and gaze at the rock sadly. How could killing Ambu possibly help her remember him? She now wished that she had broken her promise.

Her family could not understand what had happened to her. Her father who doted on her was the most worried. But her mother, a more practical sort of person, said, 'Don't worry. She is growing up. Children sometimes need space and quiet to think. Let her be.'

When she had to return home, she would walk by where she had buried Ambu the eel, and cry. Her tears watered the ground where he was buried. After a few days, Cheenu noticed a sapling at that spot. She was thrilled. Over a period of time, the sapling grew into a magnificent tree with a long trunk like an eel's body and many long leaves on the top—like fins that helped it breathe. It swayed in the breeze and the leaves whistled beautiful melodies. There were big fruits at the very top. Cheenu was happy again. She felt like Ambu was back. She would spend hours sitting under the tall tree.

One day, a few of the fruits fell down. When she shook them, she could hear water splashing inside. Was it the lake's water? With a big knife, she figured out how to open its thick outer covering. Inside, she saw a brown shell with two dark eyes. Eyes that reminded her of her dear friend, Ambu, the eel. She broke the shell and drank the sweet white milky liquid inside and felt refreshed. She looked out at the lake and realised Ambu was right. This tree was the best gift she and her family could get. They used the dry leaves to rebuild their hut's walls and roof, used the nut for its sweet flesh, the water to drink and the husk too. And every day she blessed Ambu for his precious and selfless gift.

My late grandfather, whom I called Velliachan (elder father), was full of stories. He would tell us these stories as we sat outside on the low wall in the thodi (front and backyard) in the early evening as he walked in the flower garden, or as we sat in the living room around the villakku (oil lamp) during the unavoidable power cut, as moths buzzed around. Most of his stories were about our family and hometown, and sometimes a folktale. "How the Coconut Tree Came to Be" is one such story. Velliachan was like any other grandfather in the world totally unique. He did not have any pet names for us and believed in talking to us six grandchildren as adults. His favourite method of bonding with us, when he was not playing the fool with us kids, or telling us stories, was to take us for a ramble amongst the trees in our family home in Malappuram, Kerala.

MY WONDERFUL MUTHASSAN

Deepti Menon

If you saw a tall, slender man in a green, checked lungi ambling along the main street in Thrissur with a bag slung over his shoulder, that would be

Muthassan, which is what I called my grandfather. His snowy white hair and erect posture made him stand out even as his twinkling eyes smiled, signifying that all was right with the world. There was mischief in those eyes as he crept out of the house without Ammamma, his long-suffering wife of many decades. Often he would end up in the most unexpected places while people hunted high and low for him.

Muthassan was twenty years older than Ammamma, and over the years, she had started treating him like a child, maybe because very often he did act like one. He knew how to be carefree and how to have a good time. He had two sides to him—one side which made him devour all the books he could lay hands on, and the other which urged him to make people around him smile.

I recall the time he went to his favourite stationery shop where the staff members greeted him with welcoming smiles, as he was a regular customer. He picked up some pens, envelopes and paper clips, put them in his bag and walked out.

He had forgotten to pay for his purchases, but the salesman let him go. He would send the bill home, as he always did, where Ammamma would pay the amount with an exasperated frown.

Muthassan loved idlis. Every morning he would place three idlis precisely on his silver plate, pour coconut chutney artistically around them and proceed to eat them, chewing meticulously. 'You must chew every morsel thirty times!' he would instruct us, his grandchildren, with a smile when we gobbled down our food because we wanted to go out and play. He would wash it all down with coffee served in his long silver glass.

When I was very young, I would watch him, wide-eyed, as he took out his dentures, brushed them carefully and placed them in a glass filled with water before he went to sleep at night. It was almost like magic. For a long time I thought he did so because he did not want to swallow his teeth in his sleep.

He loved to potter about the garden, tending to his plants and trees with care. But as he grew older, he would sometimes plant seedlings one day and then dig them up the next, to plant them elsewhere. He would pick up huge stones from one end of the garden, stagger along to the other end and dump them there, and then proceed to place them back a couple of days later. One day we found him sawing away assiduously at a huge branch even as he stood right under it, unaware that it could fall on him.

Muthassan was a metallurgist by profession and had worked in the Indian Railways. He travelled extensively and instilled the love of travelling in his daughter and two sons. They would travel in the old first class bogies which were extremely comfortable and even had attached bathrooms. The children enjoyed looking out of the large glass windows, with buildings and people whizzing by. The scenery always changed from state to state. They never forgot the wonder of those memorable journeys punctuated with the interesting snippets that their father would tell them every now and then.

The journeys were made even more interesting because Ammamma would have a large cane basket filled with delicious goodies—colourful pinwheel sandwiches, tiny samosas, puri masala and an assortment of sweets, followed by fruits. Every time she opened the basket, the aroma would hit our nostrils, making us hungrier than ever. My mother followed this ritual without fail every time we undertook a train journey, and she went one step further, handing out the goodies to her co-passengers as well. The journey would end with smiles and handshakes all around.

Muthassan was born in 1900, hence he had been educated under the British. His command over the English language was remarkable. He could recite from the Bible, the Gita and the Koran. Shakespearean stanzas flowed off his tongue, as did the poems of Tennyson, Milton and Wordsworth. He had strong opinions on writing styles, and we would pore over his books, fascinated, as he painstakingly wrote witty comments alongside the text. For example, we would suddenly be astonished when we read, 'What an unimpressive character! Wonder how he turned into a hero!' Or 'This paragraph could have been written better!' Of course, the books always seemed more interesting with those thought-provoking comments in his crabbed cursive writing.

When I was only twenty eight days old, I had had my ears pierced, as was the custom in Kerala. However, as I grew up, the holes closed as I disliked wearing earrings. When I was around eight, Muthassan decided to open up the holes in a unique fashion. He took a sharpened lead pencil and started probing around my earlobe. As he delved, turning the pencil round and round, taking care not to hurt me, the hole in one ear miraculously appeared. The other ear lobe proved more stubborn and I had to get it pierced again. The net result was that I could start wear earrings again.

As Muthassan grew older, his nights grew shorter as he found it difficult to sleep. On such occasions, he would drag his ancient typewriter

onto the dining table and go tap tap tap on it all right, till our even more ancient maid would peer out blearily, and say, 'Sir, will you please stop it? I need my sleep!'

The most amusing thing that he ever did, though it didn't seem so at the moment, was to paint his tiled bathroom floor black. My grandmother's sister had come for a visit, and she had really tiny feet as she was of smallish build. She walked in unknowingly for a bath, and when she walked out, she left little black footprints, if not on the sands of time, certainly all over our white-tiled floors.

Muthassan was also legendary for misplacing things. I got the inspiration to write my first poem when he misplaced his dentures.

Grandpa's Teeth

Grandpa was in a bitter mood,
His teeth had vanished, he howled.
He went off his drink and his food,
In search of them he prowled.

Under the sofa we saw him crawl,
'Bless my soul!' is what we did hear,
'What have we here?' was the muffled growl,
As we did curiously peer.
He handed us a long-lost hat,
With a flourish he brought out a shoe,
A walking stick, a cricket bat,
A scarf adorned with a cobweb or two.
And still he delved and still we stared,
Our eyes grew large and round;
'A worthy haul!' we all declared,
When, an old medicine chest he found.
Spluttering, he made his dusty way out,
'My teeth, I haven't yet found!'
To search he sent us all about
With a lot of fury and sound!
The garden we diligently dug out
To see if he had buried them there,
Under every pot and every sprout
But we had nothing to declare.
A yell from Grandpa suddenly,

'The dog has swallowed them, it's clear!'
We peered into its mouth warily,
'Grandpa's teeth,' it growled, 'are not here!'
From morn to night hunt did we,
For dinner we finally went down
There was Grandpa, as busy as could be
His teeth intact, with ne'er a frown.
'Why, Grandpa,' we chorused all,
'Found your teeth?' we all did smile.
Grandpa sheepishly grinned at the wall,
'They were in my mouth all the while.'

I can never forget the time I had to participate in a recitation contest in school. When I told Muthassan about it, he was more excited than I was, and set out to find the perfect poem for me to learn. 'It has to have a story and romance and truth!' he said. Accordingly, I set out to learn Tennyson's "Lady Clare" by heart. Muthassan taught me how to understand the theme and recite the poem with feeling. He spent hours helping me to perfect my pronunciation. He was thrilled when I won a prize for my performance. Even today, my heart beats faster when I recite in my mind –

'If I come drest like a village maid
I am but as my fortunes are:
I am a beggar born,' she said,
'And not the Lady Clare.'

Muthassan was fascinated by clocks of all sizes and shapes. He would open them up, look into their depths and study their working. It was his duty to wind up all the clocks at home. One noon he wound up all the clocks, and promptly at twelve they all began chiming, in various tones, and we could not hear a word till they stopped. Sadly, when he passed away, the clocks also stopped their chiming, as there was no one to wind them so diligently. It reminded me of a favourite song of mine which was aptly titled "My Grandfather's Clock".

So that was my Muthassan. He lived life to the hilt, doing all the things he loved best—reading, writing, gardening and spreading sunshine with his optimism. I never heard him say a bad word about anyone.

Today, when I read a beautiful line, hear a kind word spoken or see a smile that lights up the world, I think of my Muthassan who will always live on in the hearts of his loved ones.

Dadu and the Planets

Abira Ganguli

My grandfather stood outside the door of his classroom, shivering. Not from cold. It was a bright summer day, the trees in full bloom, birds chirping and a warm breeze blowing. No, Dadu was shivering with fury. He stood facing the classroom, arms by his sides, hands shoved in his pockets even as tears of indignation and outrage rolled down his cheeks. Dadu was nine at the time.

The day had had a satisfying start with *doodh cheere*. Steaming milk, flattened rice, ripened, fragrant and soft bananas mashed together with fresh *khajurer gur* or dates jaggery from the trees that dotted Sonamukhi. Everything came from the land surrounding the village. With his tummy happy, Dadu had started for school, gently tossing pebbles on the way, talking to the trees and the clouds, ready for the day ahead.

The first two lessons continued with the same gentle pace as the morning. English, followed by Mathematics. Dadu was a sharp young boy who paid attention in class when he liked the subjects being taught. He liked English and Maths. Once in a while when things got boring, he drifted into his favourite daydream. He was a Trojan warrior in the great Greek epic, *Iliad,* by Homer. Dressed in glittering armour and brandishing his spear, he led the army to rise against the Spartans! He was just settling into a long duel with the enemy when he was jolted out of his reverie by the shrill voice of Prabhat babu.

'Sunil, might we invite you back to class? Or do you already know what I am about to teach?'

Prabhat babu was the science teacher. Even though Dadu loved Science, his second most favourite subject after English, Prabhat babu did not like Dadu. His dislike dated back to when Dadu's uncle, the district magistrate, had ruled against Prabhat babu's family in a case. Even though the ruling had been more than a decade ago, Prabhat babu and his family had never got over it. His bitterness had spilled onto the unsuspecting nine-year-old who, much to the teacher's dismay, did very well in class.

Dadu sat up straight, bright red from being picked on in front of everyone, and opened his eyes wide to make sure he zoned into the lesson.

He saw that Prabhat babu's kurta already had a few red stains from the droplets of *paan* dribble that had slithered down his chin, jumping over his throat onto his white starched kurta. However, Dadu tore his eyes away from their steady progress to look up the board where a few large circles had been drawn.

'Today we shall laarn about the Solaar Sistame,' Prabhat babu quite unnecessarily bellowed. It was a small class, in a tiny room that the primary school could barely afford. Better infrastructure awaited those boys who made it to secondary school. Dadu sat up even straighter. He loved the solar system! In fact, the planets were practically his friends! Venus, Mars and Mercury, and the giant gas planets Jupiter and Saturn. And what about those planets far far away? He knew them all. He even knew that Earth was not the only planet with its own moon.

'There are nine planets in the Solaar Sistame which revolve around our star, the Sun.'

Those were the days before Pluto had been downgraded. We still had nine planets hurtling around the Sun.

'Which is the largest planet?' enquired Prabhat babu as he squinted at the rows of little bobbing heads in front of him. Little boys in various stages of interest and disinterest, some fully engaged, scratching their scabs, others doodling or straining to keep their eyes peeled open. It was the class right before the first break of the day.

One hand shot up.

'Yes, Sunil,' he sighed. Why did this boy have to know the answers each time?

'Jupiter! The largest planet is also a gas planet. It has several moons. It's …'

'Answer only what has been asked!' Dadu was cut short by Prabhat babu. 'Or would you prefer to teach the lesson, Sunil?'

'No, sorry sir,' apologised Dadu, wishing that the ground would open up and swallow him even as he heard the smothered laughs from his classmates. They loved anything that brightened up a Monday at school.

'Jupitaar is the largest planet. It is mainly made up of gas. It is said that even if all the other eight

SCIENCE
EARTH
MOON

planets were to be put inside Jupitaar, there would still be plenty of space left. It is that big!' Prabhat babu informed the class with jubilation.

Dadu's eyes sparkled and he regained some of his excitement. This was new information. He loved learning! He effortlessly imagined all the other planets inside Jupiter, like several small rubber balls inside a huge ball, all of them rolling on their sides and bumping into each other even as Jupiter rolled around the Sun!

'Speaking of moons, who knows our Aaarth ...', started Prabhat babu.

'Sir, I think you have drawn the sizes of the Earth and the moon incorrectly,' Dadu cut Prabhat babu off.

'What!' spat Prabhat babu. 'What!' he repeated.

'Yes,' said Dadu calmly. 'The Earth is more than three times the size of the moon and here you have drawn the moon bigger than the Earth.'

Not believing what was happening, Prabhat babu whirled around, enraged, to look at the board. There they were, the two insidious circles, innocently sharing space with the Sun on the board. He looked at what he had written below each. The pest was right! He had mistakenly written "Moon" below the bigger circle. For a brief moment, he thought of ending the whole thing and just erasing and rewriting the names. But no! That would mean being humiliated once again by this family, this time at the hands of the little brat!

No, that would not do. Having taken a decision in a few seconds, when time stood still for Sunil, he deliberately turned around.

'Sunil, come here!' he ordered as he picked up his foot ruler from the desk.

'Do You Know What Happens To Students Who Disrupt Class?'

Dadu stood in front of the class, looking up at Prabhat babu. He still could not understand what he had done. He had been listening intently to the teacher and loving every minute of the class. It was only when he saw the drawings on the board and the labelling beneath them that he poined out the error, assuming Prabhat babu had just been unmindful. For a moment he had even thought that the teacher would be really pleased and perhaps even have a kind word or two for him!

'Put out your right hand,' barked Prabhat babu.

Smack! Smack! Smack!

Three cries escaped Dadu each time the ruler came down menacingly on his small hand.

'Now go back straight to your seat. I don't want a peep out of you for the rest of the period!'

Dadu looked up at Prabhat babu, angry tears welling up in his eyes. He held the teacher's gaze for a few moments and then walked out, leaving a classroom of awestruck children and a teacher behind. He walked as far as the school gates, his hands in his pockets, and then suddenly turned around, slowly and deliberately. Had Prabhat babu seen the look in Dadu's eyes, he would have probably owned up to the error of his ways. For they were shining and focussed in the determined way of a boy with a mission, in search of justice and the truth.

Dadu walked measuredly towards the classroom, his hands still in his pockets, fingering something. He went and stood right at the door of the classroom and waited. Slowly but surely the boys took notice of him one by one and turned their heads expectantly towards the teacher, greedily awaiting whatever was to follow.

Prabhat babu took some time to catch up with what was going on. Since Dadu's brief departure from the class, he had relaxed a little and gone on with the lesson with reckless abandon. Now sensing the beginnings of a disruption, he turned to the direction of the distraction. To his disbelief, *the boy was back*!

Barely had he raised his ruler and opened his mouth wide enough to shout than a tiny pebble landed at his feet. He looked down, and before he could look up again, there came another pebble and bounced off his desk. Soon there were tiny pebbles being thrown all around him, mostly missing him, but scaring him enough to make him hide his face behind his hands, cower and scream, 'HELP! HELP!'

The class, far from helping, had started to laugh, the children rocking from side to side, holding their tummies.

'I was right, sir, the Earth IS bigger than the Moon! You always pick on ME! You ALWAYS punish ME even when YOU are wrong!' screamed Dadu, tears of anger and outrage washing his face.

Soon Dadu was inside the classroom, advancing towards the teacher's desk, and Prabhat babu was retreating towards the blackboard. Then he fled altogether, his dhoti tail trailing behind him.

The Battle of Troy had been won, this time by the Trojans. Dadu slowly let out a smile, walked to his desk, picked up his school bag, and not unlike a war hero, left the classroom amidst cheers from his friends. Justice had been served by the pebbles he had collected on the road.

***

'Our home, the Aarth, is the thaard from the Sun. We are just the right distance from the Sun and get the perfect balance of heat and cold. And that is why our planet can …'

'I know, I know, that is why there is life on Earth.'

'Yes. That is how we have life on Aarth,' said Prabhat babu, ignoring the fact that the annoying Sunil had spoken out of turn this time. It was the day after the ruckus and he just wanted to get on with this class which had suddenly become tedious. Why did every class that had Sunil in it get so trying? Oh, if only his family had won that case, they would have had access to all that land, he would have been the landlord of so many people, collected rent, been so rich. Then he wouldn't have had to come to this irritating class and teach this awful subject that he hated, science, to this pest of a boy. If only he could just swat him like a mosquito …

'Our Earth also has a moon that helps in sustaining life,' said Dadu, encouraged by Prabhat babu's momentary silence as he had slipped into this little fantasy. Thus, jolted back to reality by Dadu again, Prabhat babu hurriedly drew two more circles a little distance from the larger circle that represented the Sun. Below one he wrote "Earth" and below the other, "Moon".

'The Aarth has a moon, like many of the planets do. We have one moon. It is rocky like our planet and revolves around us like we revolve around the Sun. It makes tides. Does everyone know what tides are?'

'Yes!' Most of the hands shot up in the air this time.

'That's right. They are the high and low tides we see in our seas and large water bodies. The moon's pull on the Aarth causes the water to move from one direction to the other. Now if the moon had been a little farther away or closer, or bigger or smaller, things might have been bhery different. In fact we might not have been here at all!' he hollered, glowering at the class.

'And just like we have the solaar calendar that is based on the Aarth's journey around the Sun, we have a lunaar calendar based on ...'

'The moon's journey around the Earth!' the class responded in unison. Every household had a lunar calendar. Most festivals and ceremonies took place according to the lunar month. Some parents and grandparents fasted during that time. Every child knew that in their homes the Bangla calendar was more important than the Ingreji one!

Gratified, Prabhat babu let out a relaxed hmmmph when his eyes settled on Dadu who had been thoughtfully listening to him, and once in a while glancing at the board. The pest was finally quiet. Suddenly Dadu looked straight at Prabhat babu and slowly raised his hand. Prabhat babu quickly averted his gaze and tried to get back to his lesson.

A Look, A Goat, A Family Curse

Lavanya Karthik

'Don't damage anything, stay out of trouble and do not go picking fights with the neighbours!' my grandmother said.

She peered anxiously at us from the window of the bus headed to Menapuram, where her cousin Lakshmi was marrying off her youngest daughter.

'Yes, Paati!' Cheenu and I chorused.

'Relax, my dear,' my grandfather said. 'I'll keep the children out of mischief.'

'I wasn't talking to the children,' Paati replied. 'I was talking to you!'

Thatha looked injured. I smothered a grin.

'I shouldn't be leaving you alone at all,' Paati said, frowning. 'But Lachu really needs my help with the arrangements at the wedding hall. Those witless sons of hers are no use. The caterers are giving her trouble! And that famous nadaswaram player will be coming, the one she's engaged for the reception today evening! So much to do and …'

'Don't worry, dear,' Thatha soothed her. 'Everything will go smoothly.'

'There's that look!' Paati glared at Thatha. 'No mischief, do you hear? Now remember …' Our eyes glazed over as she rattled off a long list of warnings, reminders and instructions for us to follow.

'… and don't forget …' the bus revved up at that very instant and, with a lot of rattling and squealing noises, rolled out into the road. '… the …oat!'

'What was that about a boat?' I asked, as we made our way home. 'Or was it a coat?'

'Or maybe "goat",' Thatha smiled.

'Goat. Deafeningly goat!' Cheenu yelled, swinging like a monkey from Thatha's arm. He had just turned six that month, and insisted on trying out every big word he came across. 'Definitely,' I corrected him with all the authority a nine year old big sister could muster.

'Hah! So we all agree!' Thatha said. 'Goat it is!'

'No, Thatha,' I began. He glanced at me for a second, then strode away with Cheenu hanging off his arm. I stood there, staring after them.

Had Thatha just given me The Look?

At first, second and third glance, my grandfather would have struck no one as particularly interesting or remarkable. He was small and skinny, with a shock of white hair and a lot of wrinkles. He wore thick glasses with black frames that made his eyes look enormous. He was usually dressed, despite Paati's best efforts, in crumpled khadi kurtas and baggy trousers. Like I said, utterly unremarkable.

It was only when he started talking that you realised he had a secret power—he could weave words into the most incredible stories. With nothing more than his quiet voice and his earnest gaze, he could talk an enchanted web around his listeners, convince them of the most incredible ideas and coax the most fantastic thoughts into their heads. The most hardened listener would thaw and melt under the gentle warmth of his stories, the grimmest face crack into a smile.

You'll see what I mean soon enough.

***

'Time to go, kids!' Thatha announced later that afternoon. 'Cheenu, get Bruce Lee!'

We strode out into the backyard where Thatha's pet goat stood, grazing by the hedge. Thatha had found him abandoned by the roadside a year ago. 'Poor little fellow!' he had cooed, when Paati had

Hello
MEENAPURAM
41

objected to this strange pet. 'He's barely more than skin and bones. Let him stay, dear. You'll barely notice him.'

A year later, it was difficult not to notice the goat, which had grown to the size of a small donkey and earned a reputation as a fierce and fearless fighter, always ready to take on any creature foolish enough to cross his path—dogs, cattle, even humans. He'd turned out to be the best guard dog my grandparents had ever had, especially when it came to their precious vegetable garden. Thatha, a big fan of martial arts movies, had named the goat after his idol.

Bruce Lee cocked his head at us as we approached him now, dressed in our best clothes. He was almost as tall as I was, and chewing on what looked like a chunk of tin roofing. Around his neck hung a necklace of big, knobby rudraksh beads that our neighbour Ranga had dropped in haste last week, after the goat surprised him stealing Thatha's prize tomatoes. Cheenu still fell over, giggling, recalling the way Ranga had screamed and scrambled over the hedge, leaving most of his checkered trousers behind in Bruce Lee's snarling jaws.

'He even looks like that rascal Ranga, with those beads, and those big teeth!' Thatha giggled as Bruce Lee rattled his beads and bleated at us in delight. 'Come on, boy, let's go.'

We trooped to Thatha's car, an ancient Morris Minor that Thatha tended to like a child. Bruce Lee, who liked going for drives, promptly scrambled into the back seat and settled down, his head on Cheenu's lap. I got into the front seat beside Thatha, who was frowning and fiddling with the gearstick and the brakes.

'Thatha,' I said, trying one last time. 'I don't think Paati said "goat". She must have said …'

'Uh-oh,' said Thatha.

'What?'

'The car won't start.'

'Eh?'

'The car won't start.'

'What?'

'*The car won't start*!' Cheenu roared in my ear.

We sat there in silence. Menapuram was an hour's drive from our town. What were we going to do?

***

We made it to the bus stand just as the last bus to Menapuram trundled down Market Street towards us.

'Thatha,' I huffed, gasping for breath from our sprint down the road, 'they'll never let Bruce Lee on the bus.' For Thatha had insisted we bring the goat along, as Paati had ordered. Cheenu stood by the road, his arms around Bruce Lee's neck, cooing into his twitching ear. The enormous goat gurgled in pleasure and nuzzled my brother's cheek.

Thatha looked at me. 'Leave it to me,' he smiled, as the bus pulled up beside us with a great hiss and a crash of gears.

Something flashed in his eye. The corner of his mouth twitched. His eyebrow wiggled just the tiniest bit.

It was The Look.

A look like the one he'd given me before he'd convinced my snooty cousin Suguna that packs of wild dogs were prowling the streets of the town, eating young girls with high-pitched voices. It had taken her mother three hours to coax her down from the musty old storage lofts over the cowshed.

A look like the one he'd given me before he'd convinced the mayor the great banyan tree in the centre of the market was home to ancient—and possibly bad-tempered—spirits, which is why cutting it down to widen the road would be a very bad idea. The mayor still visited the tree every new moon with flowers and incense, and held up traffic while he stood there, chanting prayers to his ancestors.

A look probably like the one, if Paati's giggly stories were to be believed, that he gave her all those many years ago, before he'd gently talked her stern, disapproving father into giving their marriage his blessing.

The Look that came before The Words.

'No goats, saar,' the conductor said, peering down at us from the door. Heads popped out of every window behind him.

'This,' Thatha said, 'is no goat.'

'It is quite a monster,' the conductor agreed. 'But still, no animals allowed.'

'This is no goat,' Thatha repeated, and his voice suddenly seemed to ring loud and clear like a temple bell. 'This is Ranga, son of Seshagiri Iyengar. He has been struck by a family curse.'

There was a moment of silence so thick you could have cut through it with a knife. Even Bruce Lee stopped demolishing a roadside shrub and looked up at Thatha with interest.

Then the whole bus erupted into loud laughter.

'Good one, saar,' the conductor gasped, wiping his eyes. 'But still …'

Thatha was already talking. His voice, quiet yet clear, rose up into the still air, working its way around his audience, weaving its web. Slowly but surely, the murmurs and giggles died away. The bus driver turned off the rumbling engine and leaned in. The conductor stood rapt with attention. Even Cheenu, usually chittering and cackling like the little monkey that he was, drew quietly to my side and stayed there.

Thatha talked; we listened.

All that existed in that moment was my grandfather's voice, as he narrated the tale of a callow youth called Ranga, descendant of a rich yet greedy man who had angered a powerful sage. The sage had cursed his family tree, and doomed every thief that graced its branches to be transformed instantly into a goat. Why, Thatha himself had witnessed the horrible transformation! His eyes grew wide in horror, his voice quavered. The crowd gasped as he described the events that occurred after Ranga had sneaked into Thatha's tomato patch in the dead of night. The crowd hiccupped in sorrow as he described the plight of Ranga's aged parents. And they murmured in approval as he told them how he, as a good neighbour, had offered to help them out by taking Ranga to the temple astrologer in Menapuram in search of a cure. I listened, as wide-eyed and open-mouthed as the rest of them, not because I believed Thatha, but because I couldn't believe how easily he'd ensnared them with his words.

No one dared speak when he was finally done. It felt like the bus and the trees and the great monstrous goat at my feet were holding their collective breath. I knew I was.

'Wait!' A voice boomed from the back of the bus. A chubby man with a great mop of oily hair stuck his head out of a window. 'Did you say Ranga, son of Seshagiri Iyengar? The one who lives in that big corner house on Gandhi street?'

'Yes,' Thatha said coolly, sizing up this unexpected development in his tale.

'I know him!' the man bellowed. 'I know him well!' He elbowed his way down the aisle and thudded down the steps of the bus.

'You do?' Thatha asked.

'Indeed I do!'

'You really do?'

'I just said I do!'

'Well,' Thatha said, 'then you should have no trouble recognising him!'

The man was taken aback for a second. Then he slowly bent over and peered into Bruce Lee's face. The goat made a loud, rumbling noise that we had come to recognise as his warning roar. Cheenu kept a tight hold of the rope around Bruce Lee's neck. I watched, fascinated. So did everyone else on the bus.

'It … looks like him!' the man remarked, staring wide-eyed at the animal. 'Those hideous teeth! Those small, mean eyes!'

He peered closer. 'And those are the rudraksh beads he always wears! He had them on when I met him last week!'

Still staring, the man slowly raised a hand to Bruce Lee's forehead.

Bruce Lee roared and snapped his teeth at the man's hand.

'My God!' the man exclaimed, falling over backwards in alarm. 'The same bad temper!'

He stood up, his hands clapped to his chest, eyes wide in shock.

'It is Ranga!' he screamed.

Things went smoothly after that. The conductor helped us onto the bus. Bags were moved and people moved to make room for Thatha and Cheenu and even poor cursed Ranga. Thatha had to politely turn away about a dozen people who offered to accompany him to the temple, saying Ranga's privacy needed to be respected. After all, if things went well, they would see Ranga in his human form soon enough. He also let slip that curses like these could be contagious.

Two hours later, we reached Menapuram.

***

Paati hurried out of the wedding hall just as we were tying Bruce Lee to the gatepost.

'You're late!' she scolded. 'And your clothes are a disgra… Oh! He's here!'

A large white Ambassador car swerved to a halt, narrowly missing us. A very large and grumpy-looking man alighted from it. He stood there by the gate for a moment, his disapproving gaze taking in our clothes, our dishevelled hair and our giant goat. Then a crowd of Paati's relatives swarmed out to greet him and lead him indoors.

'Who's that bloated fellow?' Thatha asked. 'And what a moustache! Looks like a walrus in a silk kurta.'

'That,' Paati said icily, 'is the famous nadaswaram player. Why is that dreadful goat here?'

'You a…asked us to get him,' I stammered. 'Er … didn't you?'

'I did not!' Paati snapped.

'You did, dear,' Thatha soothed him. 'As you left, you told us, "*Don't forget the …*"'

'Coat!' Paati screamed. 'I said coat! Don't forget the coat!'

'What coat?'

'The new coat hanging in the upstairs cupboard! The one the tailor delivered yesterday! The one Lachu had ordered especially for the bridegroom, to wear at the reception!'

We stood there in silence as Paati seethed and raged.

Cheenu's small, sticky hand crept up into mine. 'At least we didn't marriage anything,' he whispered.

'Damage,' I corrected him automatically.

Right on cue, we heard the sound of glass shattering.

Bruce Lee, enraged at being tied, had vented his fury on the headlights of the white Ambassador.

The famous nadaswaram player stopped in his tracks. Then he bellowed in rage and ran towards his car.

'Well, at least we didn't get into fights with the neighbours,' Cheenu said.

I thought about the reception Ranga would get the next time he stepped out of his house, but said nothing.

We heard a familiar roar. A wild scream and the frantic *slap-slap* of running feet followed.

Bruce Lee had pulled free of the gatepost and was chasing the famous nadaswaram player down the street.

'We are in so much trouble,' I sighed. 'Deafeningly in trouble,' Cheenu agreed.

Gentle hands pressed down on our shoulders. A soft soothing voice whispered in our ears, 'Leave it to me.'

We turned to look up at our grandfather—at his thin, wrinkled face and his shock of white hair and his dusty, dishevelled clothes. And there it was—in his eyes, at the corner of his mouth and in the tiniest twitch of his eyebrow—The Look.

DHRUVA

Nikita Deshpande

The shepherds watched from the fields as the poor young prince fell off his horse for the sixth time.

This time Dhruva didn't bother getting up. The smell of cool mud sticking to his cheek was strangely comforting. He lay there, listening to the bird singing from a faraway tree. 'A koel,' he thought, recognising its whistle.

'Up, up, up!' his annoying stepbrother croaked from his seat atop the king's favourite mare. 'Are you eating mud now, you big *bhains*? God! You'll eat anything.'

Dhruva spat a mouthful of mud and got up. His horse stared at its hooves, looking as though he was praying that Dhruva should not attempt to ride him again. The boy took the hint and walked away from the horses towards the palace, which was his home.

'Wh… what are you doing?' his brother came riding up beside him. 'Get back on that horse! Father has promised the court that you will ride into the palace on your eighth birthday. Like a proper grown-up.'

This stung Dhruva. But he told himself not to cry. Varun would be meaner if he cried.

‘I don’t like riding horses, Varun,’ Dhruva said in a quiet voice. ‘Clearly they don’t like me on their backs either. And anyway, I don’t want to be a prince.’

What Dhruva didn’t say was that he also did not want to be whatever it was to be “a proper grown-up”. He had a secret. One that kicked and twisted inside him every day. Varun would only make fun of him if he found out.

‘Don’t be stupid,’ Varun said, aiming a little kick at Dhruva’s side. ‘It’s these terrible clothes you wear. Riding is for men who wear leather clothes. Not stupid little idiots who like to dance around wearing their mothers’ silks.’

Dhruva ignored the jab and ran from Varun as fast as he could. The silks were more special to him than the expensive Arabian horse his father, the king, had bought him.

Dhruva had made these clothes himself, with a little help from his mother. Some nights they both sat out on the terrace, stitching and knitting and making embroideries together. He liked to tell mother the names of all the stars he knew.

For his birthday, Dhruva and his mother were working on a new dhoti and shirt, made of deep indigo silk. And they were stitching shiny rhinestones into them to look like Dhruva's favourite star patterns.

Varun raced Dhruva to the palace gates and got off his horse, an evil smile plastered on his face. He opened his arms, ready to grab Dhruva and take him back to the flatlands to finish the horse-riding lesson.

But Dhruva was clever. And in the palace, being clever meant you were faster too.

Dhruva pretended to bend down, clutching his tummy like he was tired of running. Then, before Varun could even think to move, Dhruva ran into the overgrown bushes next to the west wall.

Behind the bushes was an old tunnel that only Dhruva knew well. He locked the door to the tunnel behind him, panting.

'Guards! Soldiers!' Varun's voice came from the other side. 'Our Prince-cess has run away again!'

Dhruva's heart jumped with fear. What if Varun had guessed? There, in the dark, Dhruva said his secret out loud.

'I want to be a girl. I don't feel good about being a boy. Or a prince.' He gulped. 'I feel like I would be a good princess, though.'

It didn't sound like such a bad thing when he was alone and whispering it down into the underbelly of the old fortress.

But he felt afraid about his secret around Varun and father. 'You're almost a man now, Dhruva,' father liked to say. 'Walk straight. Carry yourself tall! Like a prince.'

Dhruva crawled in the black tunnels, feeling his way up to the palace. He had studied the maps well. He counted all the right turns until he reached a dead end. Here he climbed up the wall and pushed at a little door in the ceiling.

The door opened and Dhruva pulled himself up into the palace kitchens.

Dhruva stuffed a laddoo in his mouth and crept unseen towards his father's chambers. If only he could find Father alone and explain everything about the riding lessons!

'If Varun reaches him first, I'll be in so much trouble!' he thought.

The royal guards let him pass. Dhruva smiled. His father was curled up in a squishy armchair by the large palace windows, fast asleep. A rather long scroll of paper had fallen from his limp hands to the floor. Lengthy letters always put Dhruva's father to sleep. 'Read this for me, Dhruva,' Father would say. 'It's so long and boring.'

Dhruva told himself to be brave, like his mother. Father loved him, after all. He loved Dhruva's maps of the night sky. He loved his drawings of flying chariots.

Slowly, Dhruva climbed into his father's lap and laid his head on his father's chest. He did not worry about his mud-stained cheeks or his tattered silks.

Father opened his eyes. 'Mmm. What's this, Dhruva?'

'Father,' said Dhruva, hugging him tight.

Father's moustache curled up as he smiled. 'Why aren't you outside? At your horse-riding lesson?'

Dhruva looked down at his hands. He should tell him. He should be like his mother, who always spoke the truth, even if it was difficult.

'Father, I … I d-don't like riding horses, father,' he stuttered.

'Nobody likes it at first,' said the king. He lifted Dhruva's head from his chest and sat up straight. 'But riding is a must for princes. Someday, if you're good enough, you may ride beside me into a great war.'

'I don't like riding. I don't like h-horses. Or wars. I don't even like seeing blood, father,' Dhruva muttered.

'What is this nonsense, Dhruva?' His father's voice was sharp as the edge of a sword. 'You are a prince of the family and you will do as you are told. Your birthday is close. It is time to accept your duties as a man of the royal …'

'But I don't want to be a man!' Dhruva said. He felt brave now. 'I want to be like mother. I want to learn to dance and write poetry and sing, and I want to study science and maps but also stitching and …'

Slap.

Father's hand had struck the boy's face so hard, Dhruva fell off his lap and onto the floor.

'There is no place for you in this family,' father screamed. His red face looked like a horned demon's like the one carved into the palace gates. 'Out! Get out!'

Dhruva got to his feet and ran, as fast as he could, tears running down his face. He ran without knowing where he was going, past the gardens, past the carved demons. Someone had painted all the family Gods into the back wall of the palace. He only stopped when he reached the picture of Vishnu.

He sat down and cried.

Mother found him there hours later. He was starving, and his cheek still hurt. Mother put down a copper plate laden with ghee rotis and mango pickle and an earthen cup full of buttermilk. She sat down quietly beside Dhruva and fed him.

‘Dhruva,’ his mother said after a long silence, looking up at the portrait of Vishnu, ‘haven’t I told you the story of Mohini?’

Dhruva looked up at her. Her face was bright in the torchlight.

‘Lord Vishnu ch–changed himself into Mohini to help the Gods save the world from evil,’ he said slowly. ‘But weren’t the other Gods angry, Mother? Vishnu is a boy God. And Mohini is a girl …’

Mother’s eyes were soft. Did she know his secret too?

‘One person can be many things, Dhruva,’ she said, feeding him a morsel of pickle and roti. ‘Pray to the Gods, my son. They can give you whatever you want. But you must pray with complete faith. Never forget who you really are inside. And what you want.’

‘I want father to love me again,’ Dhruva said, without thinking. ‘I want him to give me back my place in the family.’

Mother sighed. ‘Then pray with all your might. And you will have it. Now come, let us return to the palace.’

'No, mother.' Dhruva sat up straight. 'I will wait here and pray. Until I am welcome in the family again.'

'But, my darling …'

Dhruva refused to listen. He pushed away the copper plate, sat up straight, closed his eyes and folded his hands.

His mother took it for stubbornness. One night out in the cold would teach him a lesson. But a night passed and her handmaids reported at noon that the boy still hadn't opened his eyes.

At nightfall, she went again, plate in hand, ready to talk him out of it. But her pleas and nudges had no effect on him. Dhruva sat there, still as a rock, unwilling to move even an inch.

When ten days passed, Father sent his ministers to see for themselves if the stories were really true. They told him the boy hadn't moved in more than a week.

Months passed and the seasons changed. The rains washed everything away. A chill fell over the palace. Mother stopped eating, stitching and singing. Father started teaching Varun all about his duties as the new prince.

And Dhruva still sat in his place behind the palace wall. Slowly the hair on his head grew long.

On the first morning of summer, Dhruva's eyes tightened from the unbearable heat of the sun. He opened them and saw the most beautiful sight. It was not the sun that had awakened him but the glowing body of a blue-skinned God, about twenty feet tall. She had waist-length hair and large almond eyes. Her pink lips curled into a gentle smile.

Her face looked like the painting of Vishnu behind Dhruva had come alive.

'M-Mohini,' said Dhruva, joining hands and bowing before the God.

'You have done so, so well, my child,' she said in a voice deeper and stronger than he had expected. 'Ask for anything. And you will have it.'

Her eyes were soft and they twinkled, like his mother's.

'Mother,' he said, sobbing, because it felt like he had forgotten what he had wanted from the God.

'What is it, darling?'

'I want to sit in your lap, Mother. I want to be your daughter. Your child.'

'But you are my child! My girl. Look at us. Are we not the same?'

Dhruva blinked and held out a hand, then a foot.

The tattered silks were gone, and in their place were silken skirts. Dhruva's body felt like her own. Her wish had come true. It was like the right key had suddenly twisted into place and unlocked something important inside. Finally, finally she didn't feel strange in her own skin. There was still small, fine hair on her arms but also bracelets on her wrists, shaped like lotuses and elephants.

Dhruva wept with joy. 'I want … to hug you, mother, and I want that nobody should … ever … take me away from your arms.'

Mohini smiled and got down on one knee.

'Come!' She patted her strong shoulders and put out a palm.

Dhruva put her feet in Mohini's palm. She seated her on her shoulders. Dhruva closed her eyes and smelled the jasmines in her hair. But before she could get used to it, Mohini had risen from the ground.

There was magic in the air. Mohini's shoulders turned into flanks. And as she began to run, Dhruva could hear the sound of a horse running across the grounds. When Dhruva opened her eyes, she was riding the fastest horse in the universe. They were speeding away from the palace walls, towards the fields. And before Dhruva knew what was happening, Mohini blinked. A set of large wings appeared at her sides.

This time Dhruva didn't close her eyes. She felt completely safe.

The shepherds in the field saw a giant blue horse with huge wings take flight. They swore they had seen a young girl riding the horse, her arms stretched out as if to hug the sky.

They promised anyone who would listen that a new star had appeared in the sky that night. Right where the flying creature had disappeared.

The shepherds named the star Dhruva, after their lost prince.

When others in my family told the story of Dhruva, they'd focus on the infinite power of faith in the Gods and how it could give you anything you wanted. In one version, Dhruva was thrown out of his father's lap simply because the king's younger wife wanted her son on the throne. But when my grandfather told the story, he liked to make it about Dhruva's need to make "a place" for himself. I loved how the central theme of the story changed, depending on who told it. With this retelling, I wanted to explore mythology and stories as a safe space for us to become who we truly are.

Papa Julian

Nalini Sorensen

I'm not particularly old (try telling my back that after yoga), but try as I might, I cannot remember a single story that either my Nana Flossie or my Grandma Lily told me when I was a little girl.

I can remember my Nana Flossie tying a scarf around her head, holding my hand and taking me walking to church. I can remember her giving me coins to put in the charity box near the statue of the Virgin Mary …

I can remember my Grandma Lily coughing, her metal snuff box always close at hand. I can remember her using Konkani words mixed with English …

But not one single story can I remember. Not *one*!

Both my grandmothers left this world to go on to the other side before I was even ten years old. And both my grandfathers died before I was even born. So I feel a little deprived, not just of the stories that could have been told and passed down through the ages, but also of that special connection that grandparents seem to have with their grandchildren. I look at my mum and my husband's mum spoil my sons, with just the tiniest twinge of envy, and try to ignore the fact that my mother, who was excessively strict with my brother and me growing up, defends the antics of her grandchildren. I used to roll my eyes about it, but now I mostly just enjoy it.

Recently, one adventurous day, I went tale-hunting. I'm a children's author and I'm always sniffing around for stories. Surely, even if I couldn't remember a story that had been passed down, at least my mum or dad or aunts or uncles would remember a story or two that had been passed down to them by their parents.

Right? Wrong.

Not.

One.

Story.

Was.

Remembered.

If there's one thing getting published teaches you, it's resilience. So I wasn't glum for long. I realised I may have been asking the wrong questions. I changed my questions, and lo and behold, I had a story!

***

My Papa Julian, my mum's dad, was one of three children. He had two elder sisters. The story goes that Papa Julian was a posthumous child; my great grandfather died while my great grandmother was pregnant with my Papa Julian. This was at a time when everyone longed for a boy child. (Being a mum of two boys, I honestly can't see why ... but I digress.) Through the emotional grieving and hormonal turmoil, my great grandmother would stand in the church in front of Our Lady's statue with her palao open, hands on her swollen belly, and cry and plead for a son. There were no sonographs or MRIs at that time, so when my Papa Julian, did arrive, it was like her prayers were answered, and basically party time all around.

Given the circumstances surrounding his birth, my Papa Julian was, as you might imagine, spoilt rotten from the word go. His teachers were instructed not to punish him or even pull him up under any circumstances. Homework did not apply to him; grades weren't relevant.

The home situation wasn't much different. He'd eat his sisters' share of goodies and my Nana would flatly tell the girls that it was because they should not have saved their share to be eaten later. The sense of justice in their lives was slightly skewed.

One day Papa Julien decided to cycle through a coconut grove blindfolded. He insisted on doing this, and refused to heed any rational advice from anyone around him telling him otherwise. His mind was set. He yelled, "Aoun kortholon!" (I will do it!) and just went for it with gay abandon. Albert Einstein tested gravity, my papa tested … fate. Sadly, he failed. He ended up with a huge gash on his forehead that he proudly displayed to everyone for the rest of his life.

My mum says that Papa Julian had all kinds of superstitious beliefs. If his left palm itched, he believed he would lose money. If his right one did, he believed he would receive money. Hopefully he did scratch those itchy palms.

But my mum insists that for his utterly spoilt upbringing and crazy superstitions, he was an extremely caring father. Each Saturday was "Daddy's day", when he took all five of his daughters out to the city or to "town" as my mum calls it. Gateway of India, Chowpatty beach, the zoo, the aquarium or just visiting friends or cousins who lived a few suburbs away. All five of his girls were spoilt with creamy cakes from Monginis, ginger chips and ice creams when they were with him on these outings, away from their mother's watchful eyes. The waiters were instructed to keep bringing the treats as long as the girls could eat. He apparently never interfered in his daughters' school or academic activities, just in their social ones.

There are lessons to be learnt there, I think. All his daughters today don't remember their grades and can't remember the stories he told them at bedtime. But they do remember these happy times with him; they do remember the gash on his forehead. They remember his spirit for risk and his love for living life and creating happy childhood memories for them.

As for me, I loved unearthing this bit of family history about the person Papa Julian was. I'm convinced there's a little bit of him in me, and most definitely a big bit of him in my younger son. He has a black right eye and a marvellous bruise above his right eyebrow right at this moment as proof. It's in his genes.

I can't stop smiling at the fact that the person whose mother begged and pleaded for a boy fathered five girls; no boys.

Isn't that just a little bit funny?

Sarla Must Learn

Sonali Bhatia

In the 1930s, when my aunt Sarla was a little girl, the British were ruling India.

Sarla's father was adamant that India should be a free country, and he joined Mahatma Gandhi's

Sarla was sulking. She didn't want to study. 'I'm a girl,' she protested. 'Girls don't study!'

'Now, Sarla,' her mother admonished, 'you know that your father doesn't have that mindset. You are lucky. Nobody gave me a chance to study. Take your bath quickly and get ready. Masterji will be here any moment.'

Muttering under her breath, Sarla went to the bathroom and splashed a few mugs of water over herself. She then put on her blue ghagra choli and ran to the back garden to look for her younger sister, Kamala.

'You're lucky,' she told Kamala. 'Nobody makes you study.'

'They will, when I get big like you,' Kamala replied. 'Then we can study together.'

'By that time I will be married,' Sarla laughed.

'No, you won't. Our father doesn't think the way most people do. He's going to make you study till the tenth standard before you get married.'

'Shhhh.'

They heard their mother go to the front gate to greet Masterji. The two girls quickly climbed the chikoo tree they were sitting under. 'Now Masterji won't find us,' they whispered.

'Girls, I know you're up there. Now, Sarla, do you remember what I taught you last time?'

'No, Masterji, but have a nice, ripe chikoo,' Sarla shouted back. With expert aim, she threw a fruit down to Masterji who caught it almost casually.

'Enough fooling around. Let's get back to addition …'

Sarla and Kamala were hiding again, but this time there was no fooling.

They were in the old-fashioned bathroom, with an Indian-style toilet and no flush. Both girls were quiet, their hearts beating, sweat pouring from their foreheads. They were quickly tearing paper and trying to dispose them down the toilet using a metal bucket filled with water.

The British soldiers were at the door.

Nanaji was an important part of the freedom struggle, and those papers contained the names of those who were working with him, in secret, to try and overthrow the British. If the papers were found, there would be dire consequences for Sarla's family and the families of the dozen or so people whose names were on the list. The girls' mother was at the gate, keeping the soldiers talking, while the girls were doing the vital task of making the papers disappear.

'Why are they so thick?' six-year-old Kamala whispered. 'I can't tear them properly.'

'Shhh,' replied eight-year-old Sarla. 'Help me. These bits are choking up the drain.'

The girls heard horse hooves retreating. Their mother had managed to send the British soldiers away. Their house had not been searched. They were safe, at least for now.

'Gandhiji thanked us himself,' Sarla told her friends later, 'when he heard how we had hidden quietly in the toilet and torn the papers. He told us we were brave.'

'Gandhiji did something else too, didn't he?' Nanaji's eyes twinkled.

'Yes.'

'What?' her friends asked.

'He asked me what I could give for my country,' Sarla said. 'I told him, Bapu, I have nothing to give. He pointed at my ears. He said that I had gold earrings. I took them off and gave them to him.'

'Those were inherited from your grandmother, child. They should have been in the family. I tried to buy them back from Gandhiji, but he wouldn't sell them to me!' Sarla's mother rebuked her.

'I gave them to Gandhiji!' Sarla protested. 'You should not have tried to buy them back!'

'What do you know about these things, Sarla? Anyway, now go and study. Masterji has been complaining about you!'

'Then I'll complain about Masterji.'

'No. You'll go and revise what he taught you. I want you to study well so that you can pass your tenth standard exam when you are fourteen or fifteen,' Nanaji said.

'Girls don't pass their tenth standard exam, Pappa. They put mehendi on their hands and a bindi on their forehead and wear nice clothes and shiny jewellery and get married.'

'You'll do all that after you pass your tenth standard exam. Now study.'

***

It was a big day for the Jessani family.

Sarla had, indeed, passed her tenth standard exam. The results were in the newspapers, and excited friends and family members, having looked up her candidate number and found it on the third class list had flocked to the house with mithai and flower garlands.

'Now you'll get married,' Kamala whispered, as she ate her fourth peda.

***

The rejoicing was short-lived.

A few days after Sarla's results, her mother came to the garden where she and Kamala were watering the plants.

'Girls,' she said, and immediately her daughters knew there was something wrong. They stood stock still, listening.

पू रे
ER

'Your father is nowhere to be found. He didn't reach his office this morning, and his colleagues have searched for him through the city. Nobody knows where he is.'

Those were the most agonising six months Sarla or Kamala had ever known. Was their father alive? Where was he? Was he thinking of them? Would their mother be a widow with a white saree forever? Questions haunted them as they ate, slept or did their chores.

Then one day …

'He's alive! Thank God!'

There was a message from Nanaji. He was alive but in prison, in a faraway place. The British were allowing wives to visit their husbands in the prison, and Sarla's mother had to leave immediately to take a train there. 'You know how to run the house now, girls,' she said. 'And all the servants will help you. Masterji will continue to come for Kamala. I'll be away for quite a few days. It's a long train journey.'

The girls begged to go to the station with their mother. She allowed it, knowing they wanted to be together with her for the tonga ride, telling her everything they wanted to convey to their father.

The station was crowded. Several wives of prisoners were boarding the same train. Among them were many women known to both Sarla and Kamala. They hugged their mother goodbye, promised to be good, and stood on the platform till the train was out of sight.

'We won't see mother for ten days now!' Kamala didn't know whether to be upset about missing her mother or to be full of joy at the news that her father had been found at last.

'We're big now. We'll manage.'

***

But their mother wasn't away for ten days.

In two days she was back.

The girls hugged her, but they knew, again, that something was wrong.

'Didn't you meet him, Mamma?' Kamala finally whispered.

'No. All of us were sent back.'

'Back? Why?'

'The British were allowing visits, but with a wall in between the prisoner and his wife. That means, Pappa in one room there, a wall in between, and me in another room. All the men said that this was an insult. They sent a message to us to take the next train back. We didn't even get to the halfway point.'

Their mother was trying to be brave, but the girls knew what she was feeling. Both of them put their arms around her and the three stood in silence for a long time.

They had to be brave. They had to show the British that they would hold their heads up high, and not bow down in desperation. They would make their father proud of them.

This is based on what I remember of my Aunt Sarla's true stories.

The Ghost In The Attic

Sukanya Venkatraghavan

'I think there is a ghost in the attic.'

Swami, wiry and green-eyed, whose concentration was entirely on the succulent golden mango he was eating, didn't react immediately.

Gopi, short and bug-eyed, was annoyed. He had expected more excitement from his friend. After all, ghosts in the attic were not all that common where they lived. Ghouls in banyan trees were more popular, and yakshis near the temple pond where the frangipani trees bloomed all year round were a common thing.

'Hmmm,' said Swami, now picking at a mango strand from between his front teeth.

'*Swami*!'

'Yes, I heard you the first time. A ghost in my attic. What makes you say that?'

'There are noises,' said Gopi, again pausing for effect.

This time Swami looked up, his green eyes mildly curious. 'What kind of noises?'

'Like things are being moved around. Scratchy shuffly noises.'

'And how come I didn't notice, considering I live there?'

'You sleep like Kumbhakaran. That's why!'

Swami grinned. He slept in the room right below the attic and Gopi often slept at his place.

'You should wake me up the next time you hear these noises. Also, don't tell Amma. She will say it is Ammu's ghost. And she will stop letting you stay over.'

Gopi nodded. The two fell silent as they walked home. Both were thinking about Ammu. She was a girl who had disappeared long ago and the favourite local legend was that she had drowned in the pond and was now a ghost. Except, no one had ever seen or experienced the presence of this ghost.

They reached the black and white iron gates of Swami's house when Gopi said almost under his breath, 'What if it is Ammu?'

Both boys turned their gaze towards the topmost window of the old Kerala-style house Swami lived in It had thick wooden bars on the window and nobody ever really went into that room.

'Let's go check it out now,' said Swami. Gopi gulped. He wasn't half as daring as Swami who was both spirited and ready for adventure even though this meant he got into a lot of trouble. But Swami never complained about all that. He always took it on his chin.

The boys found themselves at the bottom of the staircase. The railing was broken and full of splinters. Some of the steps, made of old marble, had chipped away. One really had to watch his step while climbing them, but Swami had no trouble with it. He usually sprinted up, two steps at a time.

'Come on,' he said, starting to climb the stairs. Gopi followed him hesitantly.

They sprinted up the first few steps and then paused at the landing.

'Can you hear it?' asked Gopi under his breath. Swami shook his head.

'I can. Can you still not hear it?' he repeated.

Swami was still. His eyes were bright and curious as he strained to hear what Gopi could. His sharp ears soon caught on to the sound.

Scratch scratch scratchity scratch … rustle rustle … whooooooshh …

‘I can hear it,’ he said, as he took a slow step forward.

Rustle rustle krruuummmkkkrrrrr kugghhhhhh …

‘Why would Ammu make a noise like that?’ asked Gopi, his voice a mere whisper now.

Swami didn’t say anything. They moved up the stairs slowly, not daring to sprint anymore.

They were outside the little room now, the attic where things not used anymore, or broken, were sent to gather dust. Forgotten things that nobody bothered about.

‘Should we go in?’ asked Gopi. The sounds had stopped for the moment. There was dead silence except for the chirping of a lizard in the corner.

‘Lizards are a sign that something supernatural is around,’ said Gopi weakly. ‘Swami …’

Swami glanced at the lizard and then at the door.

‘Sometimes the thing you are afraid of is more afraid of you,’ he muttered under his breath.

‘What are you blabbering?’ asked Gopi in a loud irritated whisper.

Swami didn't say a word. He took a step forward and slid the rusty bolt back on its socket. The bolt screeched in an unpleasant manner as flakes of rust fell off them. A spider had built cobwebs over the door, and as Swami slowly pushed it inwards, the cobwebs gave way, hanging over the door, grey and limp.

'Ammu?' Gopi's voice was high-pitched as he stood outside the half-open door.

'Ssshhhhh,' said Swami, and without warning, stepped inside the attic.

'Swami,' squeaked Gopi almost inaudibly, but bravely followed his best friend into the attic room.

They looked around. Everything old and forgotten was here. Old boxes full of broken Navaratri dolls, Appa's old bicycle, an old bed, some umbrellas, more boxes, something lumpy covered under a bedsheet …

'I don't see anything,' said Gopi.

'You can't see ghosts, you *mandoos* (idiot),' said Swami.

Gopi gulped. 'Let's go, Swami. Clearly there is nothing here.'

A long beam of light hit their bare feet. Swami's green eyes followed the light back to where it started. A broken window. He walked towards it, his feet leaving dusty imprints on the terracotta floor.

Rustle rustle scratchity scratch …

Kkkrggggghhhhh kuuurrrrrrrrr.

Swami was now at the window. Gopi's eyes were wide with fright.

'SSSWWAAAMMIIIIII … Leetsssss go …'

Swami didn't turn back or listen to him. All his attention was turned on an old uruli (brass cauldron) perched on top of a table with three legs. The fourth stump had a box propped under it.

'Swaamiiiii,' Gopi's voice was a mere whimper now.

Kkkrrrrruuuuuuu kawkawkawkawkaw …

The lizard outside chirped in tandem. Between these two creepy sounds there was absolute silence. Gopi shivered.

‘Gopi …’ Swami signalled to his friend. Gopi walked towards him, unsure and frightened, muttering the Bhagawati’s name under his breath.

He was right behind Swami when something swooped in through the window. Something black and shiny, a shape that flew in so fast that Gopi screamed. A pair of beady black eyes bored into them. And then a war cry.

KAWKAWKAW.

Something within the cauldron echoed. Kawkawkaw …

Swami was smiling. Gopi peeked into the cauldron. There was a roughly built nest there and four furry creatures reached out, beaks larger than their heads.

Crow babies!

‘There’s your ghost,’ grinned Swami. ‘Your ghost is a crow.’

Gopi looked sheepish.

‘This crow has one white feather, see,’ said Swami, pointing to its wing.

Gopi had had enough. Ghosts, crows, crow babies, attics, noises …

'They look creepy enough,' he said, sulking. As they left the room of forgotten things, Swami chuckled and the crow spread her wings over the cawing babies protectively.

***

'AMMA … Fooood …'

Swami and Gopi had dashed in straight from the temple. Amma, Swami's mother, looked at them out of the corner of her eye. Swami swiped a banana off the kitchen table and bit into it.

'Sit down. I can't feed you just yet. I have to feed Ammu first.'

Swami almost choked on his banana. Gopi stared at him and then at Swami's mother.

'Aa-a-Ammu? What do you mean, Mami?' he spluttered.

'Ammu, the crow,' said Amma. 'I am convinced it is her. When she was a little girl she used to come around every day just in time for lunch.

Your grandmother would feed her. Then she disappeared, poor thing. In any case, we must feed the crows before we eat. They could be the dead returning to meet us. It is a very old and respected tradition.'

She placed a small mound of rice, plain dal and ghee on a ladle and offered it to the picture of Lord Krishna hung on the wall before walking over to the window.

'By the way, what were both of you doing in the attic yesterday? Don't think I didn't see you creeping up the stairs. Aaah … there you are!'

Something black and shiny appeared at the window. It looked at Swami and Gopi out of knowing black beady eyes. Amma placed the contents of the ladle on the window sill, muttering, 'Eat, Ammu. You always liked ghee and rice …'

Swami and Gopi watched in silence as the crow glanced at them before taking a beakful of rice, dal and ghee and then spread out her wings, lifting off towards the attic, its one shiny white feather glinting in the sunlight.

Stories about my grandfather TB *Swamination are the stuff of legends. With this one, I have pieced together a tale that could be true or a figment of my imagination.* He *was known to be a rebel, daring, and always looking for adventure. If there had been a ghost in his attic, I have no doubt he would have gone looking for it.*

KOKI

Supriya Sehgal

'We're an unlikely breed of Punjabis,' my mother says with a furrowed brow.

'Our wiry arms and spindly legs don't give away our roots,' she grumbles, trying to wrap a sari around my stick-like frame. When I stand back for her to inspect the last twenty minutes' effort, she gently slaps her forehead with her palm in frustration. 'Go wear a salwar below the petticoat. It'll give you some kilos in the right place. I used to do it all the time.'

Even in the bustle of a family wedding, there is ample opportunity to swerve into conversations that take us decades back in time. My older aunts corroborate my mother's claim of being a thin, bespectacled, wormy girl who wore two salwars to look a reasonable size. They jostle to look at their own heavy-set frames in the only slim mirror in the room, and giggle at how they barely fit.

Someone brings in steaming cups of extra sweet tea, and everyone takes a break from silks and silver. We all slump down on the bed, wrapping our fingers around the cups to beat the chill of a January evening in Jaipur. The conversations drift from Udaipur, where the siblings bundled up on black cycles to watch Bollywood movies, to the snowy evenings of Shimla. These details have been discussed so vividly that without having been there, I feel, for example, Biji's (grandmother) harsh reprimand to the cleaning lady. I can visualize exactly what the sunny courtyard at the Delhi home looks like. My uncle steps in to join in the banter and we are back to a story that all of us love. A story about my mother, Koki. My uncle is my mother's brother, elder to her by fourteen years. An octogenarian, he is the only person in our family who has a vivid memory of partition.

August 1947. For some, the cusp of independence and freedom. For others, the beginning of a forever-fractured relationship between two communities that would fester in hearts for generations to come. It was the year when India and Pakistan were shaped from the political aspirations of a handful. Over the years, the rhetoric offered by the media and the leaders of both the nations might have become increasingly divisive, but heartening stories are still plentiful. On both sides of the border.

These stories are undiluted by politically fuelled flare-ups, when the country was a wonderful amalgam of two dominant religions that offered undeniable cultural wealth. My favourite story is how Koki was born and how Khota Sikka played such an important part in this episode.

The streets of Sialkot were burning. Muslim rioters were out in the streets and had been dragging out the Hindus to set them on fire. Rumours were rife that a gang had already reached the neighbouring areas. Paralysed with fear and dread, my grandfather sat with his gaze cemented to the door—waiting for it to be slammed open anytime. My grandfather's was the only Hindu family in a Muslim colony for over twenty years. So integrated were they with the neighbours that the eldest daughter of the family sometimes donned a burkha to step out with her Muslim friends. Having never felt a shred of intimidation, this was not easy to fathom.

The door did open, but it did not slam. On the contrary, it creaked open discreetly, and in walked Khota Sikka (Hindi word used for an defective coin). It was my postmaster grandfather's careless subordinate who he often chided. 'You are useless. A khota sikka,' he would say in a stinging tone. Weighed down by a pile of burkha, one for each member of the family, he entered and spoke in whispers. He had managed to arrange for a horse cart that had to be loaded immediately, so he could transport the family to his own house, close to the border near Amritsar. In his house the family would be safe. Khota Sikka was a Muslim. Choking on tears of gratitude, my grandfather rounded up the most important things from the house, locked the door for the last time and helped everyone up the horse cart. For weeks they took refuge in Khota Sikka's home, keeping a low profile by not even stepping onto the verandah.

The evening of the 29th of August was a stifling one. The summers veiled the northern parts of the country in blistering heat and

suffocating humidity. The refuged family huddled inside a dark room while a fiery mob sat in the courtyard of the same house, planning to "finish the postmaster". The loudest in the group was Khota Sikka, whose courtyard was the nerve centre for planning the riots, building teams to burn down homes. His cry for revenge against the Hindus trumped others easily. In front of his Muslim neighbours, Khota Sikka feigned anger, resentment and a desire to kill the enemies. While the murder was being planned, my mother blubbered her first coos under a thick blanket, borrowed from the mastermind's wife. Despite the stress of fleeing home, my grandmother gave birth to the youngest of the five, Koki. Many weeks later, Khota Sikka managed to bundle up the family and send them safely across the border to Amritsar.

My uncle smiles wistfully and chuckles to shatter the rapt attention that we've all been listening with. 'Ever since, Koki has been my favourite. Even though we are 14 years apart, she's always been my accomplice. In all games, making fun of people, coming up with limericks.'

Then, turning to his own wife, who he calls "horizontally challenged", he breaks into a rhyme that he dedicated to her when he first met her. He winks at my mother, giving her the credit for its conception.

Toh we totadiya, Tota ha samandar da
Paani pee we mundar da, Chittee chaddar kaake di
Kaarka khilaniya aa, Chaar chhale paani aa
Ik challa patla, Patle di patlayee
Navi parjaee ayee, Pinge te bithayi
Pinga gaya tut, Pabhi gayee rus
Pabhi kehndi eeeeeeeeee

Translated as -

Oh parrot! [clapping hands]

The parrot that belongs to the sea [which is ridiculous in itself]

Who drinks water only from the temple
The small boy's white sheet [referring to a younger brother or nephew]
Let me feed the kid
I'm wearing four rings
Of which one is very thin
My new sister-in-law has come home
We asked her to sit on a swing
The swing broke
The sister-in-law got offended
And she said 'Eeeeeeeee'.

The room erupts in thunderous laughter.

Yo to Yoga

Vibha Batra

I woke up in the middle of the night. Okay, fine, it was seven in the morning. For me that's the middle of the night. I opened an eye to take a peek. The shuttered green windows were closed, the room dark. I knew the sun was shining outside, just as I knew Babuji was doing yoga.

He never skipped a session. Ever. Said it was the best way to stay fit. Now Babuji was old (he was my Mom's dad, so you can imagine exactly how old), but he sure was the fittest person around. I mean, I'd never seen him ill, not once, and I was ten years old. So I guess he'd a point.

Did I say "doing" yoga? Sorry, he was practising yoga. Sounds funny, I know. As if yoga is some musical instrument we could practice. Besides, Babuji didn't need any practice … he was PERFECT. I mean, he could do the toughest of yoga poses like this. Headstand? Easy-peasy. Handstand? Cool. Backward bend? No problem. But, according to Babuji, perfection was a journey, not a destination. Sighhh!

I must have sighed louder than I thought I did, because Babuji's cheerful voice interrupted my thoughts. 'Pratah swasti!'

at was hindi for good morning. That was ow we greeted each other. Babuji always said as important for family members to speak to ch other in the mother tongue.

'Pratah swasti,' I mumbled back. 'Uff … all that noise!'

The Pujo holidays were on. So were the loudspeakers. There were two big pandals opposite Nani House and every morning they played spoilsport by playing songs at full blast.

I groaned and covered my ears with my pillow as "Shongi, Aamaar Shongi", the latest chartbuster from a Bengali movie, blared out.

Babuji shot me an amused glance. 'Now that you're up, how about giving me company?'

'Yoga?' My eyebrows shot up. Just peering over the edge of the bed to talk to him was making me giddy.

Babuji patted the floor. It's … how do you say it …' He paused, searching for the right word, before clicking his fingers. 'Easy-peasy.'

I tossed the covers aside, scrambled out of bed and plonked myself down next to his yoga mat. 'Easy for you, you've been doing, er … practising it for years.'

Babuji being Babuji knew why I was hesitating, of course. It was too much work for the holidays.

'Trust me, once you learn how to do it, you won't be able to stop,' he said in a reassuring voice. 'It will become like brushing your teeth and bathing, a part of your daily routine.'

All that twisting and turning, bending and bowing? Every. Single. Day. Phew! I just couldn't imagine doing all that, and people said I'd a vivid imagination.

'Okay, tell you what—practise it for three weeks.'

That was an awfully long time. I opened my mouth to protest.

'Three weeks and no more,' Babuji cajoled, 'and see what happens.'

'Why three weeks?' I stalled for time. 'Why not one or two or four?'

'Some people—wise people, mind you—say that's how long it takes to form a habit.'

Who could be wiser than Babuji? I wondered. He was the wisest person I knew. He was a professor and he'd written tons of books. There were always people—relatives, family friends, neighbours, poorv chatr (former students)—dropping by at Nani House to seek his help, advice and guidance on everything under the sun.

'Hmm ...' I exhaled deeply, not entirely convinced. 'I don't know ...'

'Think about it. You could show a few poses to your friends, you know, when school reopens,' Babuji suggested mildly.

My ears pricked up. Babuji had uttered the magic words. I'd love to show off, er ... show yoga poses to my friends. Puja was learning how to play the guitar, Madhu had started tennis lessons. What was I doing? Beating cousins in Poori Eating competitions. Here was an opportunity to learn something new and cool.

There was just one teeny thing I wanted to clarify before signing up for these yoga lessons. 'Will you wake me up early every morning?' I asked, a genuinely worried expression on my face.

'I won't,' Babuji promised solemnly. 'But I can't say the same for the loudspeakers,' he added, his eyes twinkling.

I rolled my eyes as another song threatened to shatter our eardrums.

'So, we're on?' he asked over the noise (pollution).

I shrugged. 'I guess.'

'Great!' Babuji beamed. 'Get the spare mat—it's right there in the corner.'

'What, NOW?' I asked, my eyes widening in shock.

'Why not?' he shot back. 'No time like the present, right?'

Whoa! I had thought I was going to start tomorrow or the day after. I mean, sometime in the near future. Certainly not right away!

'B-b-but what about breakfast?' I stammered. Hungry rats were playing kabaddi in my stomach.

'Yoga's practised on an empty stomach, remember?'

My face crumpled. I hadn't thought things through. But it was too late to back out.

'Come on,' Babuji said enthusiastically, 'it will be fun.'

I didn't know about fun, but how hard could it be, I wondered, rolling out the yoga mat?

It was very very VERY (to the power of thousand) tough.

And it took me only about fifteen minutes to figure that out.

'B-b-babuji?' I puffed and panted as I tried to hold the Tree Pose, failing miserably. In five seconds, my knees were like jelly and I was toppling—much like a tree in a storm—to one side. 'Can we go back to tilting our necks left and right, wiggling our toes and stretching our arms, please?'

'Those were warm-up exercises,' Babuji chuckled. 'Okay, now try this. It's known as the Warrior Pose.'

He stood straight with his legs a couple of feet apart and raised his arms to the ceiling.

I tried, but within seconds, went back to the Mountain Pose. As in, stood rooted to the spot.

Other standing poses followed. Chair, Dolphin, Triangle. By the time we reached Downward Facing Dog, I was looking like a sad puppy indeed.

'It's okay.' Babuji ruffled my hair, noting my glum expression. 'No one expects you to master it in a day.'

'A day?' I burst out. 'It's going to take me a lifetime!'

Babuji's eyes twinkled. 'Perhaps that's why it's called "practising" yoga.'

I flopped down on the mat. 'Can we puhleeeeeze take a break?' My arms and legs were groaning in protest. To say nothing of my rumbling stomach.

'Sure,' Babuji agreed with a genial smile.

The corners of my mouth lifted.

'Right after the seated yoga poses,' he added.

The corners of my mouth went back to drooping.

Fifteen minutes later, my back and stomach had joined my arms and legs in killing me.

'Okay, now breath in.' Babuji continued in a soothing voice. 'Bring both your knees to your chest, press your thighs on your abdomen, like this … hold the pose for a few seconds.'

A few breathless seconds later, I gave up and rolled off to one side. 'I c-c-can't,' I gasped.

'You can,' Babuji insisted. 'Let's try again.

Boy, was I relieved when we moved on from the Gas Relief pose!

Alas! The other poses were no better. I collapsed in the middle of the Bridge Pose, sank as Babuji demonstrated the Boat Pose, wilted during the Lotus Pose, and did anything but hee-hee while attempting the Monkey Pose. And Babuji hadn't even got to the stomach exercises.

Oh, the torture he put me through, gently yet firmly egging me on, refusing to let me give up! Even when my muscles were squeaking in protest. Even when I was falling flat on my face.

‘Think about how good you’ll feel when you finish the session.’

‘*If* I finish the session,’ I muttered.

‘That’s it …’ I vowed after the Bow Pose (Or was it the Cobra Pose?). ‘Never again … it’s the absolute last time I’m doing this …’

I was about to roll over and act dead as a dodo when Babuji asked me to do precisely that. Play dead. I warmed up to the Corpse Pose instantly. Babuji had saved the best for the last.

‘Lie flat on your back, close your eyes, legs comfortably apart, arms slightly away from your body … keep your limbs loose … take your attention to different parts of your body …’

That’s all I heard. Because, after that I dozed off!

I woke up, god knows after how long, only to find a circle of curious faces staring down at me.

‘She’s learning yoga,’ the cousins muttered, something like envy and admiration in their voices.

I sat up straight and looked past them. Babuji was at his desk, which doubled as his study. I stretched out a hand. Several hands reached for it and pulled me to my feet in one smooth motion.

I trooped up to Babuji. His face was lit up with delight, joy and something else. Pride?

'How do you feel?'

Like I'm dying. The words were at the tip of my tongue. But funnily enough, I was feeling just fine. Hungry maybe (but then, I was always hungry), but not any of the other things: exhausted or uncomfortable or sick.

'So, what do you think?' he asked, his eyes shining with excitement.

I pretended to consider for a moment.

'I think I'll be back for the next session,' I squealed, throwing my arms around Babuji's neck and hugging him tight.

'Wait till we get to the pranayaams, breathing exercises …' he began eagerly.

I drew back in mock horror. 'Uh-oh. Did I speak too soon?'

Babuji threw his head back and laughed his trademark laugh.

BONUS GRANDMA STORiES

Once Upon A Sage

Menaka Raman

Once upon a time (as all grandmother's tales must start) there was a wise sage. He lived an austere life on the banks of the river Cauvery in a simple ashram. A few thatched huts stood here and there and he was assisted by a handful of faithful disciples who lived with him.

Every day the sage would leave the ashram for a purifying bath in the river. One day, as he crossed the threshold of his ashram, a black cat darted across his path. Now, a cat crossing your path as you left your home was considered a terrible omen. And a black cat, why, that was even worse! The sage was horrified as to what effect it might have on his prayers and penance. So he began to lie in wait to catch the cat before stepping across the threshold. He would then tie it up by the ashram gate every morning before he left, and then set it free when he returned.

Time passed and one day the sage decided that it was time for him to go on a pilgrimage. He was getting older with each passing day and felt that if not now, he might never get to see the gopurams and dvajasthambas of the famous temples of the land.

The next few months went by in preparations. But every day, as always, when he left for his morning bath, the sage caught and tied up the black cat only to set it free when he came back.

The day before he left for his pilgrimage, the sage gathered his disciples around him. They loved their guru and were sad to see him leave. But they understood the importance of this journey and how much it meant to him. They listened to their guru's instructions. After detailing all that needed to be done regarding the daily prayers, rituals and customs, the sage shared one last piece of advice.

'Whatever you do, do not forget to tie the cat every morning. That is most important.'

The disciples found this instruction of their guru odd, but out of deference to his wishes, agreed to it too.

The next morning, the guru left the ashram before the sun rose. His disciples bid him goodbye and wept tears as he walked away. He turned around to look at his ashram one last time and then set off.

The guru travelled to each and every corner of the country in search of salvation, from Meenakshi temple in Madurai to the famed Padmanabhaswamy temple in Thiruvananthapuram to Lord Tryambhakeshwar's abode in the west. His sojourn took him from one great place of worship to another. Remember, there were no trains or cars or buses or planes then. The sage walked barefoot and took rest at roadside shelters or the homes of pious souls who were happy to give alms and shelter to one so devout.

Ten years passed in this manner and soon the sage found his worn feet carrying him back home. He found himself on the worn path that led to his ashram.

But what was this? The once peaceful forest surrounding his ashram was now filled with the sound of children laughing. Was that a cow he heard mooing?

The sage approached the ashram and could not believe his eyes. The once sparsely populated area with just two to three huts and little else now had ten huts. Children ran happily throughout the yard. A large cowshed was in the back and the air was heavy with the smell of hay and cow dung. Young women were busy tending to the shed, cleaning the yard and cooking the day's meals. The guru's disciples who had been lean young men when he left were now weighed down by round bellies.

The disciples caught sight of their guru and came running to greet him. They ushered him in, sat him down and soon a delicious meal was laid out before him. The disciples had many questions for their master which he answered patiently while he ate.

The master then washed his hands and sat down.

'I have answered all your questions; now I have one for you.'

'Ask us, guruji!'

'What happened to the ashram? It has changed so much in these last ten years. How did that happen?'

The disciples looked sheepish and were silent.

'It is all because of your instructions, guruji,' one of them blurted out.

The guru who had once been quick to lose his temper in the past had mellowed considerably over the years. He was bemused.

'I? I told you to do this?'

'Well, not directly. But this is all because of the cats,' piped another man.

'The cats?' the guru asked, puzzled.

'Yes. You asked us to tie up a cat every day at the entrance of the ashram. So we did. By the end of the first week, we had four cats in the ashram,' the man replied.

'And they needed milk. So we bought some cows,' another shared.

'Soon the cows had calves. And they needed looking after. So some young girls came to tend to them and look after the premises.'

There was a slightly embarrassed silence.

'Well … and then we married the girls. And soon we had children … and well, now this is what you see.'

The guru felt something warm on his foot. He looked down and saw a small black kitten. He smiled and picked it up. How strange that a bad omen could lead to something so good!

My grandparents were both storytellers. Though my grandfather was the professional playwright, it was my grandmother who always regaled us with wise and witty tales like this one. She often said there were two ways of looking at this story. One was that we shouldn't blindly follow sayings about bad omens. Another way of looking at it, she would say, is that certain beliefs and traditions have been followed for centuries for religious reasons. However, over the course of time, people then take those same rituals and twist them to mean something else, perhaps for their own convenience. Deepavali, Pongal and other Hindu festivals are today mostly seen as an occasion to eat, have fun and get together with family and friends. The religious significance is often left on the side.

Set in Stone

Kiran Manral

Long ago, long before I was born, there was a story about some people in a distant village called

Dorihaat, near Chaukutiya, back in Uttarakhand. I've never been there, to that village, but I've heard this story often enough. My mother told it to me, and people who've been there have told me about it. So I know it is true.

This is a story about a mother-in-law and her daughter-in-law. Back in those days, the menfolk went to the cities to work and the women stayed back in the villages and tended to the fields. Entire villages had no men, because all the able-bodied men went off to the cities and returned only at the time of the harvest. And so it was that this mother-in-law and daughter-in-law were in sole charge of their rice field. It was a huge field, and only the two of them were available to work on it. It was their only source of income. In the village there is no work available except farming. Everyone grows their own vegetables in their backyard. Farming is what people do as their main occupation. It is hard work, growing rice. Growing anything is hard work, of course, but rice needs one to grow the seedlings and then transplant it to the fields. And in the villages everything back then needed to be done by hand. This was a long, time-consuming process and needed a lot of stamina for it to be done manually.

It was a huge field, and the task before the two of them was daunting. But these were hardy hill people, village folk used to hard manual labour all their life, and they were not about to slack off just because it was a huge field and a lot of work. For you and me, having always lived in a city, it is unimaginable, the amount of back-breaking work that these women would need to put in their field. But for them, it was par for the course. They had done it before and they would do it again.

On the day of the transplanting, they woke up early, as they always did, before the first rays of the sun had split the sky into pale pink, orange and yellow, before the birds stirring from their nests began their chirping, before the rooster had taken his head out from beneath his wing and begun his officious task of rousing the world to its daily routine.

The mother-in-law and the daughter-in-law were determined to complete their task before the end of the day. As was the norm, they decided that they would divide the labour between themselves. The mother-in-law would do one half of the field and the daughter-in-law would do the other half, and they would meet at the centre of the field when they were done. Even though the mother-in-law was much older than the daughter-in-law, she was still relatively young because she had been married off very young, and had many years of hard work in her yet.

'We have a long day ahead of us, buari,' said the mother-in-law, as she lit the stove and fed in the twigs and sticks to make it burn to a merry flame so they could cook a meal to carry to the fields. She was a matter-of-fact woman, sensible and caring, in a gruff maternal way. She was waiting for her daughter-in-law to give her a grandchild she could play with.

'Yes, Ijja,' replied the daughter-in-law, her skin still unwrinkled despite the years of being out in

the sun, which had crumpled her mother-in-law's skin into parchment. She picked up the pail and went out to the cowshed where she milked the sole cow they had. She would keep a little of the milk for the house and take the rest to the big house in the village where they gladly accepted the surplus and paid her a bit for it every month, even though they had enough of their own cows to give them milk. They did this because they knew how difficult it was for the two women to keep body and soul together through the long months between the sowing and the reaping. She walked out to the village, moving swiftly, the anklets on her feet jingling merrily. She was joyous because she had just received a postcard the other day from her husband, telling her he would be home for a few days at harvest time, and she was giddy with anticipation of his return. Her mother-in-law was happy too. It had been far too long since she had seen her son.

It was just that bit chilly in the early morning, even though winter was far, far away yet. But that was how it always is in the mountains. It is chilly all the time. Some people get into their sweaters at the end of September and get out of them only at the end of May.

They were wearing their long-sleeved blouses and their swirling ghagras and chunnis which they kept draped on their heads for demureness when they were not working; even the mother-in-law who had long passed the age where demureness was essential. When they reached the field, they would tie the chunni onto their heads to keep their hair off their faces and to prevent the chunni from slipping off their shoulders.

By the time the daughter-in-law had returned from delivering the milk, the mother-in-law had gotten their humble meal ready for the day. They ate a quick breakfast of rotis with plain sabji and achar and tied the rest of the rotis, cooked over the open flame, along with pickle and onions, into a rough bundle. This was to be their humble meal for the day.

'Come, let's hurry,' said the mother-in-law, 'or the sun will get too high and we will be tired before we begin.'

They set off, walking at a brisk pace. The sun was still below the eastern horizon. They reached their field in a short while. When they did, the mother-in-law went right into the centre of the huge field and asked her daughter- in-law to follow her. There, in a little clearing, on a rock, she placed the little bundle of rotis and pickle and onions and told her daughter-in-law, 'You begin work from the eastern end of the field, and I will begin work from the western end, and when we meet in the centre of the field, we will have our lunch.'

The younger woman nodded in assent, and went off to the extreme end of the field. It was a huge field, and when they looked up, they couldn't see each other. The sun climbed up higher into the sky, and it got hotter. Occasionally a cool swift breeze blew and some stray clouds would sprinkle a few droplets of water and then disappear. The two women worked and worked, and the daughter-in-law sang a bit as she worked, both their backs bent, a gunny sack over their heads to protect them from the rain and sun, and the day passed. At some point the singing stopped. The transplanting remained incomplete. The two women didn't make it to the centre of the field. When the villagers realised that they hadn't returned home in the evening, they made a search party and went out to find them. Perhaps a leopard had dragged them away, they feared. All they found were two rocks in the shape of two women on opposite sides of the field. And in the centre, where they had agreed to meet to have their meal, there was no bundle with rotis and pickle and onions, but instead, there was a huge boulder.

No one could lift the stones or the boulder. They were embedded in the earth. Grown men tried. Young boys tried. The stones moved when you tried to move them with your little finger. They shook a bit but didn't budge from the spot they were embedded in. To this day, those stones lie in that field. Immobile. Silent. Relics of a day where two women struggled to finish working on the vast expanse of an entire field by themselves but didn't survive. They didn't make it to their lunch.

This is a retelling of a story from grandma Leela Manral to grandson Krish Manral.

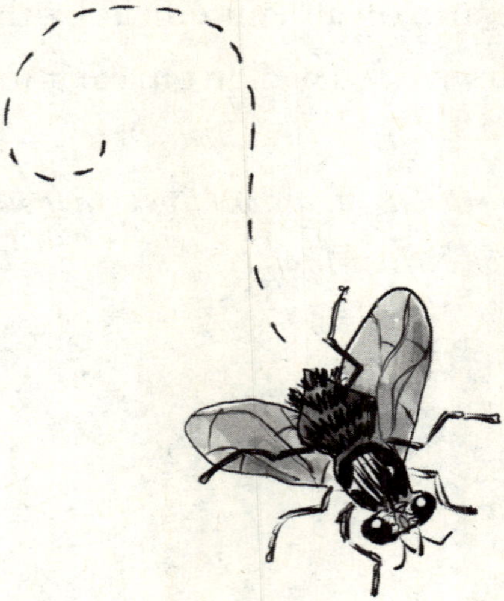

OF ABSENT-MINDED FLIES AND STUPID CROWS

Sailakshmi Deepak

A mother and a son were sitting at their window sill and having their afternoon tea. The boy saw a housefly and asked his mother what it was called.

Instead of telling him what it was called, she told him a story.

The Absent-minded Fly

Once upon a time, there lived a housefly who forgot his name. When he flew around the farm, he met a plump little calf and asked her, 'Oh plump little calf, what is my name?'

She said, 'I don't know, but maybe you could ask my mother!'

He flew to the cow and asked her, 'Oh mother of the plump little calf, what is my name?'

She said, 'I don't know, but maybe you could ask the cowherd!'

He flew to the cowherd and asked him, 'Oh cowherd who cares for the mother of the plump little calf, what is my name?'

He said, 'I don't know, but maybe you could ask my stick!'

The fly then flew to the stick and asked, 'Oh stick that is held by the cowherd who cares for the mother of the plump little calf, what is my name?'

It said, 'I don't know, but maybe you could ask the tree that I was taken from!'

He then flew to the tree and asked, 'Oh tree that gave the stick that is held by the cowherd who cares for the mother of the plump little calf, what is my name?'

It said, 'I don't know, but maybe you could ask the crane that lives on me!'

He then flew to the crane and asked, 'Oh crane that lives on the tree that gave the stick that is held by the cowherd who cares for the mother of the plump little calf, what is my name?'

She said, 'I don't know, but maybe you could ask the pond in which I play!'

He then flew to the pond and asked, 'Oh play-pond of the crane that lives on the tree that gave the stick that is held by the cowherd who cares for the mother of the plump little calf, what is my name?'

It said, 'I don't know, but maybe you could ask the fish that live inside me!'

He then flew to the fish and asked, 'Oh fish that live in the play-pond of the crane that lives on the tree that gave the stick that is held by the cowherd who cares for the mother of the plump little calf, what is my name?'

It said, 'I don't know, but maybe you could ask the fisherman who catches us!'

He then flew to the fisherman and asked, 'Oh fisherman who catches the fish that live in the play-pond of the crane that lives on the tree that gave the stick that is held by the cowherd who cares for the mother of the plump little calf, what is my name?'

It said, 'I don't know, but maybe you could ask the earthen pot that is in my hand!'

He then flew to the earthen pot and asked, 'Oh earthen pot that is in the hand of the fisherman who catches the fish that live in the play-pond of the crane that lives on the tree that gave the stick that is held by the cowherd who cares for the mother of the plump little calf, what is my name?'

It said, 'I don't know, but maybe you could ask the potter who made me!'

He then flew to the potter and asked, 'Oh potter who made the earthen pot that is in the hand of the fisherman who catches the fish that live in the play-pond of the crane that lives on the tree that gave the stick that is held by the cowherd who cares for the mother of the plump little calf, what is my name?'

It said, 'I don't know, but maybe you could ask the mud in my hand!'

He then flew to the mud and asked, 'Oh mud in the hand of the potter who made the earthen pot that is in the hand of the fisherman who catches the fish that live in the play-pond of the crane that lives on the tree that gave the stick that is held by the cowherd who cares for the mother of the plump little calf, what is my name?'

It said, 'I don't know, but maybe you could ask the grass that grows on me!'

He then flew to the grass and asked, 'Oh grass that grows on the mud in the hand of the potter who made the earthen pot that is in the hand of the fisherman who catches the fish that live in the play-pond of the crane that lives on the tree that gave the stick that is held by the cowherd who

cares for the mother of the plump little calf, what is my name?'

It said, 'I don't know, but maybe you could ask the horse that eats me!'

He then flew to the horse and asked, 'Oh horse that eats the grass that grows on the mud in the hand of the potter who made the earthen pot that is in the hand of the fisherman who catches the fish that live in the play-pond of the crane that lives on the tree that gave the stick that is held by the cowherd who cares for the mother of the plump little calf, what is my name?'

The horse just grinned and said, 'What is your name!' He laughed aloud, 'EEEEEEEEEEE!'

The fly was so happy and grateful when the horse told him his name.

The Stupid Crow

There was once an old lady who made fresh vadais (savoury doughnuts) under a tree in the village. A crow hopped up to her and cried out in hunger, asking for one vadai. The old lady tried shooing him off, but the crow did not relent. She finally gave him one vadai, and the crow flew with it to a nearby tree and was just about to start eating it.

A cunning fox was passing by and saw the crow up in the tree. The fox's mouth watered for the vadai. He said to the crow, 'You have such beautiful eyes, your feathers shine so bright in the sunlight, your beak is so perfectly shaped.' The crow was so flattered, he stopped eating and looked at the fox, waiting for more praises. The fox then said, 'You must definitely have a beautiful voice to match your looks. Why don't you sing me a song?'

The crow, eager to impress, opened his beak and started cawing. The vadai fell to the ground and the cunning fox quickly picked it up and ran away.

The crow sadly flew back to the old lady and asked her for another vadai. When she asked him what had happened to the first one, the crow told her the story of the cunning fox. The old lady asked the crow to be careful this time, and suggested he place the vadai below his foot before singing. The cunning fox saw the crow up in the tree with another vadai. The fox flattered the crow again and asked him to sing a song. The crow placed the vadai under his foot and started singing loudly. The cunning fox then said, 'Such a beautiful song! It would be lovely if you could dance to the tune of the song, dear crow!' The crow, eager to impress, hopped around the branch. The vadai fell to the ground and the cunning fox quickly picked it up and ran away.

The crow flew back this time for another vadai and the old lady shooed him off, saying he was too stupid to be given more chances. And that the world should know that he is not the cleverest bird, after all.

Loving unconditionally, spoiling rotten and cuddling endlessly, grandparents are the best part of childhood. When the parents are busy providing and keeping house, it's the grandparent who offers the much needed warmth and relief from all the pressure. I was lucky to have at least one pair when I was growing up. We travelled to my maternal grandparents home every summer, and I remember spending many of those afternoons sprawled on Maamiammai's (that's what I called Grandma) nylon mat (paai), listening to many such Thatha-Paati (Grandma-Grandpa) stories that sounded magical only when told by them.

AUTHOR BIOS

Abira Ganguli

Abira Ganguli grew up with the love and stories of two grandfathers who sowed in her the seeds of humanity, compassion and enquiry. This story is of her maternal grandfather who was a professor of English. Abira lives and works in New York with her husband.

Asha Nehemiah

Asha Nehemiah is a popular author with children from 3 to 12 years of age. Wonderfully funny characters get into crazy adventures in her stories. Her books for children have been translated into Hindi, Tamil, Bengali, Assamese and Urdu. *Granny's Sari*, *The Rajah's Moustache*, *The Mystery of the Secret Hair Oil Formula*, *Trouble with Magic* and *The Adventures of Mooli and the Blue-Legged Alien* are some of her books for children.

Binu Sivan

After a rather short stint (a week to be exact) in an investment company, Binu Sivan found her calling as a writer of news reports, interviews, features, scripts, blogs, poems, short stories and a book on Dubai. She is currently working on her first novel.

Deepti Menon

Deepti Menon has always loved the written word. She is the author of three books, the latest being *Shadow in the Mirror*. Many of her short stories have seen the light of day in myriad anthologies. She has also worked as a freelance journalist and brought out articles in many publications.

Kiran Manral

Kiran Manral is the author of eight published books and some short stories. She is a TEDx speaker, mentor and a columnist.

Lavanya Karthik

Lavanya Karthik lives in Mumbai where she writes and illustrates children's books, eats a lot of chocolate and takes a lot of naps. She is the author of several picture books and the hilarious Ninja Nani series.

Menaka Raman

Menaka Raman is an occasional writer, runner and mother of two. She enjoys eating chocolate after her children have gone to sleep.

Nalini Sorensen

Nalini Sorensen is a children's author who loves spending time with children and looking at the world through the wonder of their eyes. She wishes she never grew up sometimes, and happily nurtures the child in herself. She is the author of *While You Are Sleeping*, *The Star That Saved the Day*, *Dada's Useless Present*, *Alphabet Dress-up* and *Number March*.

Natasha Sharma

Natasha Sharma enjoys writing picture books for tiny ones, early chapter books and early to middle grade historical fiction. Her poems have featured in anthologies, magazines and course books for schools. She has published sixteen books for children, including *Razia and the Pesky Presents* that was awarded a SABA Book Honour 2016 and *Bonkers*! that won the SCBWI Crystal Kite Award 2014 for Asia and the Middle East.

Nikita Deshpande

Nikita Deshpande writes poetry, essays, copy and screenplay, and has assisted filmmakers on films like *Fukrey* and *Mirzya*. Her debut novel *It Must've Been Something He Wrote* is a romantic comedy published by Hachette India.

Sailakshmi Deepak

Sailakshmi Deepak was born in India, raised by a village that lived under one roof called home. Her conversations in childhood were made of words, stories, anecdotes, and songs of yore. She now lives in Dubai with her two sons, husband and a dog. She volunteers at the library, at literature festivals, and loves reading, for herself and to the boys. But her favourite hobby is to constantly look for hobbies that keep her mind, body and soul happy.

Sonali Bhatia

Sonali Bhatia is a freelance writer. She's also a freelance teacher, and a Harry Potter quizmaster. She is glad to have given up a "steady job" as an advertising copywriter to do literary workshops for children as it's much more satisfying.

Sukanya Venkat

Sukanya Venkat is the author of the novel *Dark Things*. She has worked with publications like *Filmfare* and *Marie Claire* in the past and is currently cooking up her next work of fantasy

Supriya Sehgal

Supriya Sehgal is a travel writer and editor with words in over 35 books for Lonely Planet Guidebooks, Roli, Times Books and others. She contributes regularly to national and international travel publications. It's a good thing that she likes the road, as she spends more than half the year on it. Find out more on supriyasehgal.com.

Vibha Batra

Vibha Batra is an author and advertising consultant (among other things). She writes for children, young adults, adults, and senior citizens. Clearly, she's adopted a "why spare anyone" approach.

EDITOR'S BIO

When her cat is off her mouse, Lalita Iyer enjoys writing for little people and big people and the little people in big people. She has worked in advertising and journalism and been a teacher, but the cat is still the boss. She is curious about grandparents and grandchildren and the bond they share and she has had some wonderful ones. She wonders how is it that grandparents often get things done that she can't. (Chiefly involving the cat.)

Some of her books for grown-ups are: *I'm Pregnant, Not Terminally Ill, You Idiot!* and *The Whole Shebang*. For children, she has written *The Boy Who Swallowed a Nail and Other Stories* and edited *Grandma Tales* (which you must read if you loved *Grandpa Tales*).

ILLUSTRATOR'S BIO

Vidya Gopal is an illustrator based out of Bangalore. In a previous life she used to work on huge spreadsheets but now she spends time intensely gazing out of windows in search of a subject to illustrate, a story to tell. Her illustrations of everyday things and sketchbook accounts where nothing much really happens can be found under her Instagram handle - spink_bottle.

Another book in the series -